D0781905

# Rage/Killian

# Also From Alexandra Ivy

GUARDIANS OF ETERNITY
When Darkness Ends
Darkness Eternal
Hunt the Darkness
Embrace the Darkness
When Darkness Comes

MASTERS OF SEDUCTION
Volume One
Masters Of Seduction Two
Reckless: House Of Furia

ARES SERIES
Kill Without Mercy

BAYOU HEAT SERIES
Bayou Heat Collection One
Bayou Heat Collection Two
Angel/Hiss
Michel/Striker

BRANDED PACK
Stolen and Forgiven
Abandoned and Unseen

DRAGONS OF ETERNITY
Burned by Darkness

SENTINELS
On The Hunt

# Also From Laura Wright

MARK OF THE VAMPIRE
Eternal Hunger
Eternal Kiss
Eternal Blood (Especial)
Eternal Captive
Eternal Beast
Eternal Beauty (Especial)
Eternal Demon
Eternal Sin

BAYOU HEAT SERIES
Raphael & Parish
Bayon & Jean-Baptiste
Talon & Xavier
Sebastian & Aristide
Lian & Roch
Hakan & Severin
Angel & Hiss
Michel & Striker
Rage & Killian

WICKED INK CHRONICLES *(New Adult Series- 17+)*
First Ink
Shattered Ink
Rebel Ink

CAVANAUGH BROTHERS
Branded
Broken
Brash
Bonded

MASTERS OF SEDUCTION
Volume One
Masters Of Seduction Two

INCUBUS TALES

SPURS, STRIPES and SNOW Series
Sinful in Spurs

# Rage/Killian

## Bayou Heat Novellas

## By Alexandra Ivy & Laura Wright

1001 Dark Nights

EVIL EYE

CONCEPTS

Rage/Killian
Bayou Heat Novellas
By Alexandra Ivy & Laura Wright

1001 Dark Nights
Copyright 2015 Debbie Raleigh & Laura Wright
ISBN: 978-1-940887-654

Foreword: Copyright 2014 M. J. Rose
Published by Evil Eye Concepts, Incorporated

All rights reserved. No part of this book may be reproduced, scanned, or distributed in any printed or electronic form without permission. Please do not participate in or encourage piracy of copyrighted materials in violation of the author's rights.

This is a work of fiction. Names, places, characters and incidents are the product of the author's imagination and are fictitious. Any resemblance to actual persons, living or dead, events or establishments is solely coincidental.

# Acknowledgments From the Authors

To Our Readers, Current and New: We love you! Enjoy your Pantera. Grrrrowl.

Sign up for the 1001 Dark Nights Newsletter
and be entered to win a Tiffany Key necklace.

There's a contest every month!

Go to www.1001DarkNights.com to subcribe.

As a bonus, all subscribers will receive a free
1001 Dark Nights story

*The First Night*
by Lexi Blake & M.J. Rose

# One Thousand and One Dark Nights

*Once upon a time, in the future…*

*I was a student fascinated with stories and learning.
I studied philosophy, poetry, history, the occult, and
the art and science of love and magic. I had a vast
library at my father's home and collected thousands
of volumes of fantastic tales.*

*I learned all about ancient races and bygone
times. About myths and legends and dreams of all
people through the millennium. And the more I read
the stronger my imagination grew until I discovered
that I was able to travel into the stories... to actually
become part of them.*

*I wish I could say that I listened to my teacher
and respected my gift, as I ought to have. If I had, I
would not be telling you this tale now.
But I was foolhardy and confused, showing off
with bravery.*

*One afternoon, curious about the myth of the
Arabian Nights, I traveled back to ancient Persia to
see for myself if it was true that every day Shahryar
(Persian: شهريار, "king") married a new virgin, and then
sent yesterday's wife to be beheaded. It was written
and I had read, that by the time he met Scheherazade,
the vizier's daughter, he'd killed one thousand
women.*

*Something went wrong with my efforts. I arrived
in the midst of the story and somehow exchanged
places with Scheherazade – a phenomena that had
never occurred before and that still to this day, I
cannot explain.*

*Now I am trapped in that ancient past. I have taken on Scheherazade's life and the only way I can protect myself and stay alive is to do what she did to protect herself and stay alive.*

*Every night the King calls for me and listens as I spin tales. And when the evening ends and dawn breaks, I stop at a point that leaves him breathless and yearning for more. And so the King spares my life for one more day, so that he might hear the rest of my dark tale.*

*As soon as I finish a story... I begin a new one... like the one that you, dear reader, have before you now.*

# Legend of the Pantera

To most people the Pantera, a mystical race of puma-shifters who live in the depths of the Louisiana swamps, have become little more than a legend.

It was rumored that in the ancient past, twin sisters, born of magic, had created a sacred land and claimed it as their own. From that land was born creatures who were neither human or animal, but a mixture of the two.

They became faster and stronger than normal humans. Their senses were hyper acute. And when surrounded by the magic of the Wildlands in the bayous of Southern Louisiana, they were capable of shifting into pumas.

As the years passed, however, the sightings of the Pantera became so rare that the rumors faded to myths.

Most believed the entire species had become extinct.

Then months ago, they'd been forced to come out of the shadows when it was uncovered that a secret sect of humans have been experimenting with Pantera blood and DNA.

It's a battle for the future of the puma-shifters.

One they dare not lose.

No matter what the cost.

# Rage

# Chapter 1

The Wildlands were exactly what most people would expect for a pack of puma-shifters. Thick foliage, towering cypress trees, narrow water channels clogged with water lilies and banks of sweet-smelling azaleas.

A glorious, untamed bayou that stretched for miles.

But it was much more than a vast swamp. Behind the magical barriers were hundreds of comfortable homes, a state-of-the-art medical clinic, a village green where the Pantera shared meals, and a large, Colonial-style structure with black shutters that looked like it'd been plucked out of *Gone With the Wind*.

The building was currently being shared by the heads of the various factions. Suits, who were the diplomats of the Pantera. The Geeks, who took care of everything high-tech. The Healers, who could usually be found at the clinic. And the Hunters, who were the protectors.

Inside, the HQ was buzzing with activity. No big surprise. Over the past few months they'd endured a crazy-ass goddess, a traitor, and now a human corporation, Benson Enterprises, who'd been secretly kidnapping Pantera and using them as lab rats.

Which was why Rage should have suspected that something was up when Parish led him to a back room that offered them a temporary privacy.

The two male Hunters looked similar at a glance. Both had deeply bronzed skin and dark hair, although Rage kept his cut short. And both had broad shoulders and sculpted muscles that were covered by worn jeans and T-shirts, despite the chill in the air.

But while the older Parish looked like a lethal killer with scars that bisected the side of his angular face, Rage was blessed with the features of an angel. Even more fascinating, his eyes were a stunning violet that was flecked with gold.

Women had been sighing in pleasure since Rage hit puberty.

It took a closer look to see the predatory cat that lurked just below the surface.

At the moment, he looked every inch the deadly Hunter. His eyes glowed with power and if he'd been in his cat form, his tail would have been twitching as he paced from one end of the room to the other.

"No," he growled. "No, no, no."

"I'm sorry." Parish folded his arms over his chest, the air prickling with the force of his authority. The older male wasn't the leader of the Hunters because of his sparkling personality. "Did you think that was a request? Because it wasn't."

Rage grimaced, deliberately leashing his instinctive aggression. He'd discovered at an early age he could use his natural charm to…encourage people to see things his way. It was only when his cat was provoked to violence that it was obvious why his faction was Hunter instead of Diplomat.

"Please, Parish," he soothed. "Send someone else."

"There is no one else." Parish narrowed his golden eyes. "In case you missed the memo we've been having a few disasters lately."

"Exactly. I should be out searching for the mysterious Christopher," Rage said, referring to the head of Benson Enterprises, the shadowy corporation that was responsible for stealing Pantera, as well as vulnerable humans. "Or at least hunting down the Frankenstein labs. We still can't be sure we've burned them all." He pointed toward the window that overlooked the manicured grass of the communal area. Below them a few Pantera mothers were sharing a late lunch while their cubs tumbled across the spongy ground. It was winter in the Wildlands, but the Pantera embraced the brisk air. "Hell, I'll even spy on the military. Someone needs to discover who can and can't be trusted in the human government."

Parish looked far from impressed by his logic. "Are you trying to tell me how to do my job?"

"Christ, no. It's just…"

Parish frowned. "What?"

Rage hesitated. This was the first time he'd ever questioned a direct order, but there was no way in hell he wanted to deal with Lucie Gaudet.

The female Geek had been a few years younger than Rage, and growing up he'd initially felt sorry for the half-feral creature who'd lived in the outer parts of the swamp. She'd slunk around the edges of town with her hair matted and tangled, and her face covered in dirt. Almost like a fabled wood sprite who flitted among the trees, spreading mist and magic

But as they'd matured, his pity had changed to annoyance.

Instead of growing out of her odd preference for the shadows, she'd continued to lurk at a distance, and worse, she'd used her cunning intelligence to torment others. Including himself.

A born troublemaker.

"I'm a Hunter, not a Geek," he finally muttered. "Why doesn't Xavier send one of his own people to track down the female?"

Parish's lips twisted. "Because, like you, they're terrified of Lucie."

Rage scowled. "I'm not scared of her."

"No?"

The two predators glared at one another before Rage, at last, heaved a resigned sigh.

"Okay, I'm scared of her," he admitted. "She's a psycho bitch."

"She's not psycho. She's just…" Parish struggled for the word. "Misunderstood."

"Being misunderstood is shaving your head and drinking so much elderberry wine you puke purple for three days," he muttered, ignoring Parish's snort of amusement. Okay, it was possible that Rage had done both of those things. "Lucie burned down her grandfather's cottage."

Parish shrugged. "No one was inside it."

"She stole my diary so she could decrypt my private thoughts and posted them in the community center." Something that still aggravated the hell out of Rage. He'd written highly sensitive information about the various females he'd been dating at the time. All of them had refused to talk to him for weeks.

"You shouldn't have been such a hound dog," Parish said with blatant lack of sympathy.

"I wasn't a hound dog," Rage protested. "I just adore women."

Parish rolled his eyes. "A lot of women."

"Not as many as most people think," Rage retorted. It was true he spent a large majority of his time with females, but it wasn't about sex. Or at least, not everything was about sex. More than a few of his dates had been nothing more than two friends enjoying an evening together. "But I'm not ashamed of my appreciation for the opposite sex," he continued. "I love their scent. Their feel. Just having them near."

"Then why were you so upset?"

*Because she made him look like an idiot.*

He didn't share the sense of mortification he'd never forgotten.

Instead, he folded his arms over his chest.

"What about the fact that she hacked into the Pentagon?"

Parish met him glare for glare. Predictably, he refused to back down.

"Xavier took care of her lack of judgment."

"By denying her access to computers?" Rage shook his head. It was a wonder she hadn't gotten every Pantera tossed in the brig. "All that did was give her a reason to leave the Wildlands so she didn't have to follow the rules."

Parish leaned against the edge of the heavy walnut desk, the wood creaking beneath his considerable weight. Pantera had denser bones and muscle than humans.

"None of us liked following the rules. I remember you breaking them more than once."

Rage couldn't argue. He was a hell-raiser when he was young. But he was an amateur when compared to Lucie.

"I wasn't on the FBI most wanted list," he muttered.

Parish studied him for a long, nerve-wracking moment, then he grimaced, as if coming to an unwelcomed decision.

"You're not being entirely fair, *mon ami*," he abruptly said. "Life wasn't easy for Lucie."

Rage frowned. Parish was the master of the understatement. If he said life wasn't easy, then it must have been hell.

"I know her parents were Suits and spent most of their time away from the Wildlands," Rage said, struggling to recall what little he knew about the secretive female.

"Too much time away." Parish shook his head, his jaw tight. "Lucie should have been raised in the community nursery, but her grandfather insisted that she live with him."

Most cubs spent at least some time in the nursery. It helped to solidify their sense of pack. And children of Diplomats spent more time than others. The Wildlands were far safer for the cubs.

"He was a recluse, wasn't he?" Rage demanded. He barely remembered the cantankerous old man. The only time they'd crossed paths, the bastard had threatened to have Rage and his friends tossed in the bog if they ever stepped on his property.

"Unfortunately. None of us realized that he'd been affected by the rot that had already seeped into the Wildlands." Parish glanced toward the window where the lush beauty of the bayou hid the fact that only a few weeks before there'd been a creeping evil that had threatened to destroy the Pantera. "Not until too late."

Rage took a step toward his friend. "What do you mean, too late?"

"When Lucie was born, she was undersized and dangerously frail. If the Healers had been allowed to treat her, she would easily have outgrown her weakness, but Theo was determined to use what he called old magic to cure her."

Rage arched a brow. "What the hell is old magic?"

The air heated with the force of Parish's sudden burst of anger. "We assumed he meant the traditional herbs and potions from the elders. None of us knew he was tying her to trees during the middle of the night like she was a fucking rabid animal, or forcing her to hunt for her own food when she was barely old enough to shift. Lucie's early life was a brutal lesson in survival."

A savage sense of guilt twisted Rage's gut.

"Shit," he rasped, hating himself for not taking the time to find out why Lucie had always remained an outsider. And why she'd felt such an intense need to rebel.

Maybe if he'd thought about something beyond his own wounded pride he could have...

Rage abruptly leashed his cat as a growl rumbled in his chest.

He might want to taste blood, but Theo was dead and Lucie missing. He couldn't change the past. All he could do was make sure that he didn't leap to conclusions again.

"Cut her a break when you find her," Parish broke into his dark thoughts.

"*If* I find her," Rage muttered, accepting he'd been efficiently manipulated into going after the missing female.

As if there'd ever been any doubt.

Shoving away from the desk, Parish reached to lay a hand on Rage's shoulder. "I have every faith in you, *mon ami*."

"Fan-fucking-tastic," Rage muttered. "Do you have any clue where I should start?"

"New Orleans."

\* \* \* \*

The office overlooking the Mississippi River had the hushed elegance that came from money.

A lot of money.

Not that Lucie was impressed with the contemporary style. The sleek glass and steel desk was a ridiculous statement of fashion, not function. And the low leather seats couldn't possibly be comfortable. Not unless you were a contortionist. Not to mention the fact that the original oil paintings that lined the white walls looked like someone had tossed a can of paint at that canvas and called it art.

*Whatever.*

She wasn't here to be the interior decorator. Nope. She was here to give her report and get her money.

End of story.

Pacing from one end of the room to the other, Lucie waited for the man seated behind the desk to lift his head and study her with a disgruntled expression.

"How long?" he demanded.

Lucie shrugged. He was asking her how much time it'd taken her to hack into his top-of-the-line computer security system.

"Less than an hour."

"God. Damn." Vern Spencer shook his head.

The middle-aged human was no doubt attractive to most women. He had a well-maintained body, dark hair that was threaded with silver and brushed from his lean face. Currently he was wearing a designer suit that cost more than many people made in a month. His main attraction, however, was the fact he was the CEO of a billion dollar energy company. Human women seemed to be fascinated by a large bank account.

To Lucie, he was another job.

"I spent a fortune on our latest upgrades," the man groused.

"It's good, but not good enough." She nodded toward her report that he'd spread across his desk. "I've made suggestions of where you need to shore up your security." She allowed a rare smile to touch her lips. "And my bill."

"Another damn fortune," Vern grumbled, his gaze lingering on her delicate features before they moved down to her slender body that was hidden beneath a pair of jeans and faded Pat O'Brien's tee.

"Do you want the best or not?" she demanded.

"Yeah, yeah." A cunning expression touched the man's thin face. "I'll have the money transferred into your account."

Lucie rolled her eyes. She was always very clear about her demands before taking on a new job.

"You know I run a cash only business."

Vern shook his head, leaning to the side to open his briefcase. Then, grabbing a thick envelope, he tossed it onto the desk.

"You're a pain in the ass, you know that Lucie?" he asked her, watching as she snatched up the envelope and promptly counted the crisp bills inside.

She didn't trust anyone. Period.

"I try." She strolled toward the nearby door. "Let me know next time you upgrade."

There was the sound of Vern hastily rising to his feet. "What's your hurry?"

Lucie's steps never slowed. "It's late."

"Not that late. We could have a drink or—"

"No."

"What about a quick trip to Paris? I have my jet on standby—"

"No."

There was a strangled sound of disbelief. No doubt Vern was accustomed to women who would do backflips at the chance to go out with him. Like another male that she'd once known.

Bleck.

"Well, you're nothing if not blunt," he said with a small laugh.

"It saves any misunderstandings." She glanced over her shoulder, her ponytail swinging. "Call me if you have a job."

Without giving him time to press his invitation to linger, Lucie headed out of the office and toward the nearest stairs. It didn't matter she was on the tenth floor. There was no way she was going to get into an elevator.

There mere thought of being trapped in a small box made her breath lock in her lungs.

After her grandfather…

No. Lucie gave a shake of her head and jogged easily down the stairs. There was no past.

Only the future.

Within minutes, she was out of the building and moving down the dark street. Her thoughts were still with the easy money she was shoving into her back pocket. It was crazy, really. She'd started hacking in defiance of Xavier and his stupid rules. She hated people telling her what to do. Besides, being able to break into systems that were supposedly impenetrable made her feel like a badass.

And after leaving the Wildlands, she'd needed to hack to support herself.

But in the end, she'd discovered she could earn a shitload more cash by becoming legitimate. Now companies paid her to hack into their high-security systems.

How ironic was that?

The smug thought had barely drifted through her mind when an intoxicating scent of musk had her coming to a sharp halt.

Pantera.

Shit.

Although the puma-shifters preferred to stay in the Wildlands, there were always a few roaming the city. Either to spy on the humans or to keep up on their ever-changing technology. But over the years, fewer and fewer were willing to risk leaving their homelands, and she'd become overly complacent.

Knowing it was too late, she still turned, trying to dart into the nearby alley.

She'd barely manage to take a step when arms were wrapping around her waist and she was being pulled against a hard, male chest.

"You're a hard girl to track down," a low, disturbingly familiar voice whispered in her ear, sending Lucie into an instant panic. Kicking backward, she managed to connect with his shin while at the same time she turned her head, snapping her teeth at his face. "Shit, Lucie." His arms tightened until she could barely breathe, let alone move. "Easy, for god's sake, it's me."

Yeah, like she didn't know that it was Rage who held her?

This male had once figured into her every girlish fantasy. She'd spent hours watching him from a distance, fascinated by his male beauty and the easy charm that made him a favorite among the females.

And much to her embarrassment, she still found herself searching for him during the rare occurrences she returned to the Wildlands.

Now she was desperate to get away from him.

"Let me go, Rage," she growled.

He chuckled. "Long time no see."

Lucie didn't know what bad juju had crossed her path with this male, but she needed to get away. Not out of fear. Xavier had removed the bounty on her head some time ago. But this male...

He disturbed her in a way she didn't fully understand.

With practiced ease she went boneless in his arms, her head sagging against his chest.

"You're hurting me," she whimpered.

"Shit. I'm sorry, Lucie."

On cue, the strong arms loosened their grip and Lucie was shoving out of his grasp and scrambling down the alley.

If she could reach the…

With a speed that shocked her, Rage had already caught up to her and was tossing her over his shoulders as he continued down the alley and onto a backstreet.

"Parish is going to pay for this," he muttered.

Lucie scowled as she pounded Rage's back. This wasn't a chance meeting?

"Parish sent you?" she demanded.

"Yes."

She heaved a resigned sigh. "Put me down."

Ignoring her command, he picked up speed, heading away from the commercial district to a quiet residential neighborhood lined with weeping willows.

"Not until we have a chance to speak," he warned.

She slammed her fist against the hard muscles of his back, nearly breaking her fingers.

"Dammit, Rage."

"Temper, temper," he teased, moving in silence despite the fact he was carrying a squirming, furious female.

Lucie made a sound of frustration. If Parish wanted something from her, why the hell had he sent this male? The leader of the Hunters had been one of the few Pantera she'd ever let get close to her. And that was only because the stubborn bastard wouldn't take "no" for an answer. He had to have suspected that she watched Rage more than any of the other males.

Or was that the point?

Did Parish assume that she would be so dazzled by the gorgeous Rage that she would fall into line like a good little Pantera?

She wanted to laugh at the mere thought. She didn't let anything or anyone control her. Not since she escaped her grandfather. But there was nothing amusing in the jolts of excitement that were streaking through her as the heat of Rage's body seeped through her clothing and his musky scent teased at her senses.

Shit. He was hauling her around like a sack of potatoes, but she was getting turned on.

She'd dreamed a thousand nights that Rage would catch sight of her lurking in the trees and rush over to grab her in his arms. And yes, there'd been more than once she'd fantasized he would throw her over his shoulder and haul her into the shadows so he could strip off her clothes and kiss her quivering body from head to toe…

Lucie heaved a groan of relief as they reached the white, plantation-style home set well away from the street that served as a local safe house for the Pantera. Circling to the backyard, Rage was forced to lower her to her feet as he placed his hand against the scanner hidden behind a potted plant. Slowly the door slid open and Rage led her into a large kitchen that was filled with a delicious smell that made her stomach rumble with hunger.

Stepping away from the male, she glanced around the room that was lined with wooden cabinets painted a pretty white. The floor was made of flagstone, and overhead, the open-beamed ceiling had dried herbs hanging alongside a set of copper pots.

A part of her itched to get out of the house that was filled with smells of home. The potpourri that was made from the Dyesse lily that only grew in the Wildlands. Rich moss that had been carried into the kitchen on someone's shoes. And that enticing scent of food that was bubbling in a pot on the stove.

Even worse was the flame of anticipation that licked through her at the realization they were alone in the house.

Dammit.

"Are you going to tell me why you kidnapped me?" she forced herself to mutter.

Rage cocked a dark brow, his gaze taking a slow, leisurely survey of her tense form.

"Kidnapped?" he drawled. "Isn't that a little overdramatic?"

She shrugged. "I was minding my own business when I was snatched off the street and forcibly brought to this house. What would you call it?"

He flashed his wicked smile. "Your lucky night."

"Ugh." She glared at him, pretending her heart wasn't racing and her palms sweating. Christ, what was it with this male? Did he have some sort of direct connection to her deepest urges? "You haven't changed."

"You have." Without warning he prowled forward, the glow of the overhead light adding a gloss to the ebony satin of his hair and shimmering in the amazing violet eyes. Slowly his hand lifted to brush over her cheek before he was reaching to tug at the scrunchie that contained her long hair in a ponytail, allowing the reddish-gold curls to cascade down her back. A low growl rumbled in his chest. "If it wasn't for your scent, I would never have recognized you."

Lucie took a shocked step backward, slamming into the cabinets behind her as she struggled to breathe.

"What are you doing?"

The scent of his musk deepened, saturating the air with his male arousal.

"There's no need to panic." He combed his fingers through her hair, as if he was savoring the feel of the strands sliding against his skin. "Unlike you, I don't bite." He leaned down to whisper directly in her ear. "Not unless you ask really...really nice."

# Chapter 2

Rage was lost in sensations.

It was crazy.

He'd spent over six hours searching from one end of New Orleans to another trying to locate Lucie Gaudet. He was tired, hungry, and pissed that Parish was wasting his skills. He should be hunting down the bastards who were responsible for capturing Pantera and treating them as their personal test animals.

But then he'd caught Lucie's scent.

He'd recognized it immediately. A fragrant, enticing musk. Like primroses. Sweet, with the danger of prickles beneath the velvet blooms. He had no idea why it seemed so familiar. As if the smell had been a part of his unconsciousness for years. Perhaps decades.

Then he'd caught sight of his prey and it felt as if his entire world had been turned upside down.

It wasn't just her unexpected beauty, although he'd been stunned at his first glimpse. Who knew that once the tangles were combed out of her hair, it would prove to be a glorious gold that was threaded with hints of fire? Even pulled into a tight ponytail, he'd known it would look perfect spread across his pillowcase. Or that her too-thin face would mature into elegant lines that emphasized the bright gold eyes rimmed with jade?

It was the lingering resemblance to a tiny wood sprite he used to glimpse in the trees. She was elusive and untamable. Like quicksilver.

And it wasn't until he caught sight of her again that he realized just how much he'd missed her presence in the Wildlands. Oh, he'd been aggravated by her outrageous behavior. And his human side had considered her a childish pest. But deep inside it was as if his cat had been waiting, always knowing that he would once again cross paths with Lucie.

The knowledge was terrifying.

Unfortunately, it didn't keep him from being obsessed with the need to touch the wary young female. Not even when she was glaring at him as if she wanted to punch him in the junk.

Stroking his fingers through the warm silk of her hair, he watched in fasciation as it brushed against the milky softness of her cheek. At the base of her throat he could see her pulse fluttering, the evocative scent of primroses clouding his mind.

He had to have a taste.

Now.

Bending down, he skimmed his lips over her forehead. The caress was light, giving her the opportunity to turn away. Just because his cat was furiously trying to get close to her didn't mean she was equally eager.

She stiffened. Was she going to shove him away?

The question was answered when she tilted her head back to give him better access. Rage didn't hesitate. With a low growl, he covered her lips in a kiss that had nothing to do with his usual skilled seduction.

This was raw and needy and way too demanding for a first kiss.

Framing her face in his hands, Rage continued to plunder her mouth, slipping his tongue past parted lips. Oh, hell. He swallowed a moan. She tasted of spring. Sweet. Wild. Thunderously unpredictable.

She shivered against him, her arms wrapping around his neck as she tangled her tongue with his.

Joy blasted through him, his cat roaring with a fierce satisfaction.

At last...

It was the intense approval from his inner beast that had him jerking his head up in shock. He'd enjoyed a variety of lovers. All of them had offered a sensual pleasure that he'd treasured and most had remained dear friends long after their intimate relationship had come to an end.

But none of them had aroused his cat.

"Shit," he breathed, nipping at her lush lower lip. "I didn't bring you here for this."

Her nails suddenly bit into the back of his neck, the tiny pain only intensifying his desire.

"You could have fooled me," she muttered.

Rage chuckled. She might spit and hiss just like she did when she was a cub, but there was no mistaking the intoxicating scent of her arousal. Or the seductive little squirm as she tried to press closer.

The movement against his engorged cock sent tormenting shocks of bliss through him.

"If you don't like it, then why are you rubbing against me?"

She tilted her head back to glare at him, the gold eyes glowing with the power of her cat.

"I don't know."

He kissed the tip of her nose, feeling an odd sense of disorientation. There was something achingly familiar about the female, even as she seemed utterly new and different.

Was it possible his cat had truly been waiting for her to grow up?

"I warned Parish you were dangerous," he breathed, intending to pull back only to find his lips stroking over the softness of her cheek and down the line of her jaw.

"Me?" She shivered. "You're the one who's lethal to females."

He buried his face in the curve of her neck, breathing deeply of her scent. "Madness."

Her nails scraped down his back. "We have to stop."

"Yes." His tongue licked a rough path along the neckline of her tee.

She hissed out a low curse. "Rage."

He squeezed his eyes shut, battling against his cat, who was ready and eager to take this female against the wall. Or on the kitchen table. Or floor…

It didn't matter that they were virtual strangers, despite having been raised in the Wildlands. Or that Lucie had obviously harbored a deep dislike for him when she was young.

Or even that he was here on a mission of utmost importance to the Pantera.

His cat wanted this female.

Period.

With a heroic effort, Rage at last lifted his head, studying her flushed face with a brooding gaze.

"Okay, I'm stopping," he muttered.

He didn't know what he expected, but it wasn't that she was going to suddenly dart beneath his arm and head toward the door.

"I have to go."

"Wait." With a swift lunge, he was standing directly in her path, shaking his head in exasperation. How many times was she going to try and run from him? "I need to speak with you."

She glared at him, tossing back the long strands of her hair as if they annoyed her. Or maybe he was the one annoying her.

"Tough, I have things to do."

"What things?"

"None-of-your-business things."

Rage heaved a sigh. Dammit. He should have kept his hands to himself. If she ran off before he could ask for her assistance, then Parish was going to kick his ass.

Not that it had been a choice, he ruefully acknowledged. Even now his fingers were twitching with the urge to reach out and touch those glorious golden-red curls.

"I told you Parish sent me, but it's Xavier who needs your help," he said, hoping to stir her curiosity.

They were all cats at heart, after all.

"He has an entire posse of Geeks," she grudgingly pointed out, unable to resist temptation. "Why does he need me?"

"They don't have your particular talents."

Her gaze slowly narrowed, the golden eyes smoldering with a dangerous heat. "You mean he needs a hacker?"

"Exactly," he agreed, grimacing as she gave a sharp burst of laughter. That couldn't be good. "What's so funny?"

She stepped forward and poked her finger in the center of his chest. "The self-righteous pricks gave me the option of throwing away my computer or leaving the Wildlands. They claimed I was an undisciplined criminal." More poking. "And now that they need my services, they suddenly aren't so worried about ethics?"

She had a point. Rage grimaced, the guilt that he'd felt since Parish had revealed details about her childhood feeling like a lead ball in the pit of his stomach. No one would blame her for telling them all to go to hell.

Unfortunately, they needed her. And it was his responsibility to convince her to forget the past.

"Things change during times of war," he informed her, not surprised when she rolled her eyes.

"Now who's being overdramatic?"

"Make no mistake, Lucie, the Pantera are under attack," he insisted. "You haven't been around much, but—"

"I know what's been happening."

Rage's brows snapped together. "How?"

She shrugged. "Not everyone considers me a leper."

"Parish?" he guessed.

Her hands landed on her hips, her expression warning that she was tired of his questions.

"Once again. None of your business," she growled.

It wasn't. So why were his hands clenching and his cat pressing against his skin with the need to get out and track down the leader of the Hunters?

*Because he was jealous.*

The simple answer sent a jolt of shock through Rage. He'd never been jealous in his entire life.

Shaking off the strange desire to punch Parish in the face, he forced himself to concentrate on the reason he'd come to New Orleans.

"Are you refusing Xavier's request?" he demanded.

She folded her arms over her chest, her expression defensive. "What if I do?"

"Then I return home and we figure out a new plan."

She hesitated, licking her lips. "I can just walk away?"

It took a second for the insult to sink in. Then fury pulsed through him.

"Christ, Lucie, what did you expect?" he snarled. "Waterboarding? A couple broken kneecaps? Thumbscrews?"

She at least had the decency to look embarrassed as she hunched her shoulders. "I don't even know what thumbscrews are."

Rage stepped back, waving a hand toward the door. Beneath his anger was a sharp-edged hurt that she would ever believe he would threaten her with violence.

"Fine. Go," he rasped, spinning away with a low curse.

He'd managed to fuck up this meeting on an epic scale. Clearly, Parish should have sent a Suit.

Expecting to hear the slamming of the door, Rage was caught off guard when he heard Lucie heave a sigh.

"Tell me what Xavier needs," she muttered.

Slowly he turned, studying her with a suspicious frown. "Why?"

\* \* \* \*

*Why.*

A hell of a question. A shame Lucie didn't have the answer.

She knew beyond a doubt that it didn't have a damned thing to do with the male who was staring at her as if she'd just crawled beneath a rock. Hell, if it was up to her, she would walk out the door and never set eyes on him again.

He was flat-out, do-me-now trouble.

She'd always sensed it, even when she'd been too young to know why she watched him. Now that she'd actually tasted his lips and felt his touch…she ached for him with a desperation that was downright dangerous.

If she had one ounce of self-preservation, she'd be running as fast as her feet could carry her.

And it didn't have anything to do with loyalty to her people. She'd put aside her life as a Pantera, hadn't she? Okay, her cat demanded the occasional trips to the Wildlands so she could shift and absorb the magic. But she was no longer a part of the pack.

They'd never given a shit about her. Why should she care if they were in danger?

She heaved a deep sigh. The only explanation was that there was a small—very small—part of her that whispered she would regret turning her back if something truly terrible happened.

"Lucie, are you just screwing with me?" Rage abruptly growled, jerking her out of her dark thoughts.

She forced herself to meet his accusing gaze, shuddering as her cat purred in anticipation.

"Tell me what Xavier needs."

"And you'll help?"

She held up a hand. Only a fool would commit to some vague request for "help." She wanted details.

"It depends on what it is."

The violent eyes smoldered with annoyance, his lips parting only to snap together as Rage made a visible effort to accept her hesitation.

"Fine." He pointed at the wooden kitchen table. "Grab a seat."

Lucie frowned, watching as he crossed toward the stove. "What are you doing?"

"I'm starving," he said, reaching into the cabinet to pull out two bowls. "I didn't have time to eat before I left so my mother sent some of her famous gumbo with me." He scooped up two heaping bowls of the spicy stew and placed them on the table. "Don't tell me your mouth isn't watering."

It was. Rage's mom was a Nurturer who'd offered comfort to the sick Pantera with her delicious cooking. Not that Lucie had ever been allowed to be consoled by the warm-hearted woman.

Unable to resist temptation, she slid into a seat and grabbed for a spoon. "Spoiled," she muttered, more than a little jealous.

Rage had been petted and adored by his mother and four older sisters.

"Probably," he admitted, cutting thick slices of bread and grabbing a bottle of wine before he returned to the table and took his own seat. "Eat."

She sent him a glare, but she readily dug into the gumbo. Her loathing for being told what to do was no match for the enticement of Andouille sausage and plump shrimp and chopped okra, all poured over garlic rice.

A groan was wrenched from her throat as the rich flavors exploded on her tongue. "It's delicious," she muttered, keeping her head down as she cleaned the bowl and soaked up the juices with a slice of bread. "I can see why everyone was so eager to taste your mother's cooking."

She was oblivious to Rage's unwavering gaze until he leaned across the table to fill her wineglass.

"Lucie, it's no excuse, but I didn't know." He abruptly broke the silence.

She glanced up in confusion. "Know what?"

His expression was somber. "About your grandfather."

With a jerky motion she was on her feet, knocking the chair over in her haste to step away from the table. Dammit. Had Parish shared the humiliating details of her childhood?

The thought was...

Horrifying.

The very last thing she wanted was this male's pity.

"I don't discuss the past," she rasped. "Not ever."

He slowly rose to his feet, regret shimmering in his eyes. "You should have been protected. We all failed you."

Lucie wrapped her arms around her waist, her mind locked against the grim memories. It was the only way to survive.

"Are you deaf?"

"I had to say it." Rage rounded the table, prowling forward even as she instinctively backed away. "I'll never forgive myself for not doing something to help."

Lucie stiffened. There was no denying the sincerity in his voice. What he felt wasn't pity for her, but guilt that he hadn't prevented her grandfather's brutality.

Oh hell. Her heart melted. She'd always been fascinated by his concern for others. Well, that and the fact he was gorgeous, charming, and sexy as hell. His ability to display such tenderness was a stark contrast to his cat, who was vicious when provoked.

But she'd never directly experienced his fierce need to protect.

It was…intoxicating.

And oh, so dangerous.

"It wasn't your responsibility," she muttered.

"It was," he countered, moving to stand so close she could feel the heat of his body wrap around her. "I'm a Hunter."

Desperately, she tried to ignore the urge to reach out and run her fingers over his beautiful face. Just to prove to herself he was real.

She needed to put some distance between them.

"And here I thought you were just another pretty face," she mocked.

His mouth twitched. "Actually, I'm pretty all over. Just in case you were interested."

"I'm not."

"The lips say no, but those eyes…" He gave a low chuckle as she lifted her hands to shove him away.

"Are you ever going to get to the point of why you brought me here?" she growled.

His teasing expression slowly faded. "If you've been in contact with the Wildlands, then you know we recently prevented a military contractor from using *Pantera* blood as a serum to create super-soldiers in the military."

She nodded. It'd been several weeks since she'd been to the bayous, but Parish had called only a few days ago to update her. As always, she refused to tell her friend where she was living, but she couldn't break all ties with him.

"I thought Stanton was dead?"

"He is, but Xavier intercepted an e-mail from one of the researchers who was working with Locke," he said, referring to the human who had been Christopher's right-hand man and responsible for building the laboratories that experimented on *Pantera* as well as humans. "The mystery man claims he downloaded the data before we torched the place."

"Do you believe him?" Lucie asked. It would be an easy claim to make.

Rage shrugged. "Impossible to say, but we can't take the risk he isn't bluffing."

"Why not contact the human authorities?"

His beautiful features tightened. "We don't know who we can trust."

Lucie snorted. She knew exactly who she could trust.

No one.

"What do you want me to hack?" She went straight to the point.

"Whoever sent the e-mail was setting up an online auction," Rage explained. "In twenty-four hours, the top bidder will receive the supposed intel."

Lucie hesitated. She had never been able to resist a challenge. Something that'd gotten her into trouble more times than she wanted to remember.

If she intended to walk away, she had to do it now.

Rage wisely remained silent, waiting for her to sort through her inner conflict until she at last accepted the inevitable. She might want to deny the Pantera as her pack, but in her blood, they were still family.

"Show me," she muttered in resignation.

Not giving her the opportunity to change her mind, Rage turned to head out of the kitchen. They walked through a large front room with molded ceilings and a sweeping staircase before they crossed the hall into the library.

Lucie glanced around the large space. It was more or less what she expected. Traditional mahogany furnishings that were arranged around the wooden floor. On the far side of the room was a deep alcove with a brocaded chaise lounge, and at the back was a marble fireplace. Her lips twitched as she caught sight of the velvet Elvis painting that was hanging above the mantle.

Someone clearly had a sense of humor.

Rage headed directly to the large desk that was loaded with high-tech electronic surveillance equipment and a computer system that would have been a wet dream for most nerds.

Lucie, however, had a setup that was illegal in most countries.

"Xavier said he'd send the info to this computer," Rage said. "It's encrypted, but he said you should be able to—" He bit off his words as Lucie slid into the chair and swiftly lost herself in the world of electronic data.

This was the one place she felt safe.

The one place where no one and nothing could hurt her.

# Chapter 3

For the next hour, Rage paced the library. From the bay window to the fireplace. From the alcove to the towering bookcases. All the time keeping a covert watch on Lucie as her fingers flew across the keyboard.

She was completely engrossed in her work, unaware that the glow of the monitor was emphasizing the delicate beauty of her face and shimmering in the fiery highlights in her golden hair.

Rage, however, was painfully conscious of her exquisite temptation.

Something that should have bothered him, not filled him with a joyous sense of anticipation.

Of course, now that Lucie had agreed to assist Xavier, his duty was more or less complete. Why shouldn't he savor the attraction that sizzled between them? His cat had already decided she was going to be his lover. Maybe even more.

He might as well enjoy the ride.

Right?

Accepting his fate, Rage made another circle of the room, only halting when Lucie at last rose to her feet and lifted her arms over her head to stretch out her tight muscles.

Rage's cat purred, wanting to lick the pale strip of belly revealed as her tee rode up.

"Whoever set this up was clever," she said.

Rage reluctantly leashed his animal. Later he could lick. And taste. And maybe bite.

"Can you trace them?" he asked.

"Yes. The auction is set up through a remote computer." She lowered her arms and leaned against the edge of the desk. "The program is designed to pick the highest bidder, and once the money is transferred to an overseas account, the payload is released."

Rage frowned. He was a Hunter, not a Geek.

"Payload?"

"The computer files he claims to have taken before the lab was destroyed."

"Ah."

"We need to go to my place."

He studied her in surprise. The last thing he expected was an invitation to her private lair.

"Why?"

She nodded toward the computer on the desk. "Right now I'm being blocked. I can access the auction, but I can't break through the firewall to get a lock on who is responsible. I need to run a trace."

"And you have the equipment to do that?"

She rolled her eyes. "Yeah, I have the equipment."

Okay, it was a stupid question.

"Do you want to take a vehicle?"

"No." She gave a decisive shake of her head. "It's not far from here. I'll call you when I've found something."

"No."

She frowned. "No?"

He moved to stand directly in front of her. "I'm going with you."

"Why?" She squared her shoulders, instantly defensive. "Do you think I'm going to try and escape?"

Rage muttered a curse, reaching out to grasp her shoulders as he glared down at her wary expression.

"I told you that you're free to go wherever you want," he snapped. Christ. He was tired of being treated as if he was a monster. "I'm asking for your help, not holding you captive."

She scowled, refusing to apologize. "Then why do you want to go with me?"

"Because I'm curious," he said. "I want to see where you live."

"And?" she prompted, easily sensing he wasn't giving her the whole truth.

He reached out to cup her cheek in his palm, his thumb brushing her lower lip. "And my cat wants to be near you."

She trembled, her eyes darkening with excitement as her own cat responded to his touch.

"Rage," she choked out, shocked by his blunt honesty.

His lips twisted. She wasn't any more shocked than he was.

"You asked," he said.

With a sharp motion, she was jerking away from his hand, her arms folding over her waist.

"Do you have to flirt with every female?"

"I would usually say yes, but this isn't flirting."

Her scowl deepened. "Then what is it?"

Hmm. Now that was the question, wasn't it?

"Hell if I know," he growled, his animal restlessly prowling beneath the surface. The beast was growing agitated by the space Lucie insisted on putting between them. "I'm hoping you can figure it out."

She sucked in a deep breath, the musky scent that filled the air revealing she was as eager as he was to get up close and personal.

Unlike him, however, she wasn't about to give in to temptation.

At least not yet.

"Let's go," she grumbled, pausing long enough to shut down the computer before she was leaving the library and heading out of the house.

Rage was swiftly at her side, his gaze scanning the darkness for any hint of trouble.

As far as he knew, there was no one who could suspect why he was in New Orleans. Or want to target him. But it was his nature to be on guard.

Especially when he was protecting this particular female.

If someone actually tried to harm her…his jaw clenched. The unfortunate bastards would discover exactly why his mother had named him Rage.

They traveled in silence, surprisingly headed toward the French Quarter. Somehow he'd expected her to have an isolated house on the fringes of town. Instead, she led him directly to Royal Street, pointing toward the house shrouded in shadows.

"That's it."

Rage nearly fell over his feet as he caught sight of the grand mansion.

Built on a corner lot, the graceful three-storied house was framed with towering oak trees. The old bricks had been painted a warm cream and there were covered galleries on both the front and the side of the house that ran the length of the porch, with lacy iron railings.

It was graceful and posh, and whispered of days gone past.

Just how much did hacking pay?

"Yep, this is it," she muttered, pulling a key out of her pocket to lead him inside the black and white tiled foyer.

He had a brief glimpse of an overhead chandelier and a hallway that led toward an inner courtyard before she was jogging up the polished wooden staircase. They bypassed the formal living room and entered what he supposed had once been called the "parlor."

She flipped on the lights, giving him the full impact of the wide room with Corinthian columns that towered toward the fifteen-foot ceilings that still possessed the original medallions. There was a priceless Parisian rug spread across the worn floorboards and furniture that looked as if it'd come out of a European palace.

Once again, he was struck by the elegant sense of history that she'd so carefully mixed with the comforts of home.

"Wow," he breathed, strolling to the center of the room.

"What?" she demanded.

"It's beautiful."

She blushed, as if embarrassed by his genuine admiration. Then pulling an envelope out of her back pocket, she moved to pull aside an antique table to reveal a safe hidden in the wall. Quickly she had it opened and the envelope stored inside.

"The wine cooler is fully stocked," she told him as she straightened, nodding toward the heavily scrolled bar that was built in beneath the mirror that ran the entire length of one wall. "Help yourself."

Rage swiftly moved to block her path as she headed back to the door. "Where are you going?"

She blinked in surprise. "My office is over the garage."

"I want to go with you."

"I..." She swallowed her protest as she met his steady gaze, no doubt seeing his cat's fierce refusal to be left behind. "Fine. Follow me."

*To the ends of the world*, a voice whispered in the back of his mind.

They left the parlor and headed deeper into the house, at last coming to the end of a hallway where they were blocked by a heavy steel door.

Rage arched a startled brow as she placed her hand on an electronic scanner and then leaned forward to type in a complex code. Only then did she pull out an old-fashion key to open the final lock and push the door open.

"You expecting a zombie invasion?" he teased as they stepped into the narrow room that was nearly overwhelmed by the stacks of high-tech equipment and monitors that looked far too sophisticated and expensive to be sold at Best Buy.

She shrugged, snapping on the overhead lights before moving to settle in front of the nearest computer.

"Not everyone is happy with the work I do." She glanced over her shoulder to toss him a startling smile. "And there is always the off chance the zombies might show up."

Rage felt as if he'd just been punched in the gut.

Christ. She had a dimple.

Reeling from the impact of her smile, Rage was barely aware of her rapidly tapping on the keyboard. Not that he would have known what the hell she was doing even if he'd been paying attention. Still, it came as a shock when she was rising to her feet and studying him with a quizzical expression.

"That should do it," she told him.

He nodded, his gaze lowering to her lips as he remembered her sweet taste of primrose.

"Now what?"

"I'm running the trace. It's going to take a while," she said with a shrug. "If you want to go back to the safe house, I'll call you when I find something."

He stepped forward, his hand lifting to lightly circle her neck with his fingers. "Are you kicking me out?" he murmured, his thumb resting against her fluttering pulse.

She instinctively tilted back her head, offering him greater access to her throat. "This could take hours," she cautioned.

His cat rumbled in anticipation. "Good."

She shivered, her eyes molten gold in the bright overhead lights. "Good?"

"We have some time to get better acquainted," he informed her.

Before she could react, he bent down to scoop her off her feet, heading back to the main house.

He didn't know exactly where he was going, but he was sure there had to be a bedroom somewhere. He wasn't going to stop until he found it.

\* \* \* \*

Lucie told herself she should protest. She hated when men thought they could grab her as if they owned her. And she certainly never allowed them to haul her around like she was some helpless doll.

But gazing up at Rage's achingly familiar face, she knew she didn't want to protest. Not when her entire body was shuddering with an eager need she couldn't disguise.

The fantasy of this male had tantalized, teased, and tormented her for years.

Could she truly live with herself if she didn't discover if he could actually fulfill her dreams?

Shutting out the tiny voice that warned she wasn't thinking clearly, she made no move to escape when he entered her private rooms and headed directly for the bed that was arranged next to the bank of windows that overlooked the inner courtyard.

She loved New Orleans, but there were times when she felt trapped by the press of buildings and narrow streets. She liked to be able to open her windows and allow the sunshine to spread over her naked body.

Bending down, Rage gently settled her in the middle of the mattress, staring down at her with eyes that glowed with the heat of his cat.

"I thought you said you wanted to become better acquainted?" she teased.

He stilled, his jaw clenching as he visibly struggled to contain his primitive instincts. His beast was clearly anxious to do more than exchange chitchat.

The knowledge sent a shiver down her spine. Her own cat was equally eager.

Unlike humans, Pantera didn't always equate sex with some rigid morality. Sometimes it was about warmth, and companionship, and pleasure.

And sometimes it was about being with the one male who stirred her on a soul-deep level.

"Do you want to go back to the parlor?" he asked. "Or if you want, we can go out for a drink."

She lifted herself on her elbows. "What do you want?"

"You." His voice was low and rough, his heat brushing over her like a physical caress. "I want you."

It was the perfect thing to say.

Holding his gaze, she gave a slow nod. "Then we stay here."

Easily reading the invitation in her voice, Rage kicked off his boots and yanked his Tulane sweatshirt over his head. Then, unzipping his jeans, he shoved them down to reveal his hard, bronzed body in its full glory.

And it was glorious.

Her mouth went dry as she studied the hard, sculpted muscles that flowed with a fascinating ease. His chest was broad and tapered to a slender waist, with a puma tattoo just below his collarbone. His arms were ripped without unnecessary bulk, and his legs were long and lightly dusted with dark hair.

A perfect male specimen.

Yum.

"A good choice." A slow, wicked smile curved his lips as he moved to crawl onto the mattress.

"You approve?"

"Oh, I approve." He lowered his head to press his mouth to a spot just behind her ear. Lucie's cat purred in pleasure. Who knew a mere kiss could be so erotic? "In fact, I'd be happy to demonstrate just how much I approve."

"It's fairly obvious," she said, pointedly glancing toward his cock that was fully erect. Her mouth watered at the thought of wrapping her lips around that broad head and sucking him deep.

She rarely performed oral sex on men. It seemed too…intimate.

But she desperately wanted a taste of this male.

"I suppose it is," he agreed in a husky voice, nipping her earlobe. "Christ, I feel like I've waited for this moment for my entire life."

Her breath tangled in her throat at his words, a bittersweet ache clenching her heart. She wanted to believe him. But while she'd dreamed of this male night after night, she wasn't stupid enough to think that he'd ever given her a second thought.

"You don't have to say that," she muttered.

"Say what?"

"That I'm special," she said. "I know there's been a lot of females."

He heaved a sigh as he reached down to slip off her shoes, then with obvious expertise he easily rid her of her jeans and tee.

"Why does everyone assume I'm some sort of player?" he groused, kneeling beside her to run a scorching gaze over her body, now covered in nothing more than a pair of lace panties.

Lucie quivered beneath the hungry gaze. "Because you are?"

"I've had a few relationships that I'll always cherish, but none of them made me feel as if I was going to lose my mind if I couldn't kiss them."

Leaning forward, he planted his hands on the mattress as he moved to settle on top of her. She sighed at the sensation of his weight deliciously sinking her into the mattress. Instinctively, she allowed her legs to widen so he could settle between them.

Lowering his head, the raven hair brushed against the puckered tips of her nipples.

"Rage," she choked out.

His tongue flicked over her nipple, the rough stroke wrenching a moan from her throat.

"It's your turn, Lucie."

She scored her nails down the smooth skin of his back. How was she supposed to think when his touch was sending streaks of white-hot pleasure through her?

"My turn for what?" she at last ground out.

He continued to tease her nipple, his cock pressing with flawless precision against her pussy. Oh…yes. It felt good. But she wanted that thick length sinking into her aching body.

"To tell me that I'm not just another male," he said, stroking a line of kisses between her breasts. "That this is different for you."

How could he doubt it? She'd never melted from a mere kiss. Or groaned with impatience during foreplay.

And certainly she'd never considered the possibility of handcuffing a male to her bed so he couldn't escape.

Of course, it seemed better not to share that particular sentiment.

"Your ego is big enough," she informed him.

Rage abruptly lifted his head, gazing down at her with a smoldering intensity. "You think this is about my ego?"

Her lips parted to give a flippant retort, only to have the words falter beneath the hint of vulnerability in his violet eyes.

Her answer mattered. She wasn't sure why, but she wasn't going to deliberately ruin this fragile moment.

"I don't know," she confessed with blunt honesty. "If you know my past then you have to realize that I don't have much experience with relationships. I don't understand the rules to the game."

With a low groan, Rage surged upward to claim her lips in an openmouthed kiss that was hard with unrestrained hunger. She could taste the musk of his cat. Feel the heat of his need blazing through her like wildfire.

Any lingering hesitation was seared away.

"This is no game to me," he whispered against her lips. "Not this time."

Her hips arched upward in blatant invitation. "Why is it different?"

"Because my cat has never been so hungry for a female."

She retained enough self-preservation to flinch at his possessive tone. The only thing in her life she was certain of was the fact that she couldn't depend on anyone but herself.

Something she was in danger of forgetting.

"Just for tonight," she warned, scraping her nails up his back. She exulted in his violent shudder of pleasure. "As soon as I'm done with the hack, you'll return to the Wildlands and I'll stay here."

"Lucie," he breathed. "Can we enjoy a few hours together before you start talking about getting rid of me?"

"I just don't want you thinking..."

She forgot how to speak as his mouth skimmed restless kisses along the length of her neck, over her breasts, and down the clenched muscles of her belly.

"Let's make a mutual promise to stop thinking," he rasped. "It's a highly overrated habit."

It was, Lucie discovered when his tongue dipped into her belly button. Why think when it was much better just to feel the shocking throb of longing between her legs, the clever fingers that knew exactly where to touch, the warm brush of his lips, the hard promise of his cock...

It was like standing in the middle of a violent inferno with no desire to avoid being burned.

"I promise not to think, if you promise not to stop," she managed to breathe.

# Chapter 4

Rage gave a low chuckle.

Stop? He was fairly certain that nothing on the face of this earth could make him stop. Not when his body was primed and ready to please this female.

Of course, he would prefer if there wasn't still a hint of wariness deep in her eyes. And that he sensed she would flee in terror if he confessed that his cat was more than just hungry for her.

That it had decided to claim her for his own.

Right now, beggars couldn't be choosers. He would take what he could get until he could convince her to accept him as her mate.

Allowing his hands to glide up her bare thighs, he grasped her panties and with one jerk, he had them ripped off her body. Only then did he move so he could spread her legs, his gaze drinking in the sight of her wet pussy.

Exquisite.

A roar of approval echoed in his head as his cat took full appreciation of her naked beauty, startling Rage. He'd never had his animal so close to the surface during sex.

It was intense and intoxicating, and viciously erotic.

With a low growl, he leaned forward to stroke his tongue through her luscious cream. The taste of primroses exploded in his mouth, clouding his mind with pure lust.

He heard Lucie suck in a sharp breath as he licked her with a growing urgency, the sound filled with the same raw need that clawed at him.

"I could become addicted to your taste," he said thickly, his hands exploring up her body to cup her breasts, his thumbs teasing her hardened nipples.

She gave a strangled groan, her hips lifting off the bed as her fingers clenched the quilt spread over the mattress.

"Rage," she moaned.

"Yes, my sweet Lucie?"

"I want you inside me."

Rage chuckled, giving her pussy a last, lingering taste before he was kissing his way back up her body. His cock was aching, desperate to give in to her command.

Not just to feel her slick heat wrap around him, but he wanted her skin to be marked with his scent, imprinting himself on her as he emptied his essence deep inside her.

Easily sensing his possessive animal instinct, Lucie abruptly set up. Rage tensed, afraid he might have spooked her with his hunger. But even as he prepared himself for her rejection, she was leaning forward to trail a path of wet, mind-destroying kisses over his chest, her hands grasping his hips as he jerked in shocked pleasure.

His cat understood it was her power play. She needed to feel as if she was in control of the encounter.

He hid a smile, willing to let her play as he planted his knees on each side of her hips. At least for now.

His brief spurt of amusement was lost as she spread the tormenting kisses, heading ever lower.

Rage clenched his teeth. Oh, hell. He was already close to the edge. He moaned, his desperation to toss her back on the mattress and enter her with one thrust tempered by the fierce pleasure of her maddening kisses.

Clearly enjoying her power over his body, Lucie used the tip of her tongue to trace a path from his bellybutton down to his balls. A groan was wrenched from his throat as she sucked them into her mouth, driving him to the edge of madness before she turned her attention to his aching cock.

"No more," he rasped as she slipped the tip between her lips. He reached down to grab her shoulders and pulled her up.

She flashed a smug smile before he was abruptly turning her around and leaning her forward, so she was on her hands and knees. Then he grasped her hips, pulling her into the perfect position.

"Rage?" Her eyes widened with shocked pleasure as he thrust forward, and with one smooth motion, impaled himself in her damp heat. "Oh, hell."

Smoothing his lips up her back, Rage sank his teeth into her shoulder, savoring her low moan of pleasure. Her pussy clenched around him, making him shudder with sheer bliss.

"Shit, Lucie," he rasped. "I'm not sure how long I can last."

Tightening his hold on her hips, Rage withdrew to the very tip before slowly sinking back into her welcoming heat. She rolled her hips at the same time and Rage muttered a curse, waging war against his looming orgasm.

Dammit. There was no way he was going to embarrass himself by coming before his female.

Quickening his pace, he reached around her body to stroke his fingers over her tender clit. The air was perfumed with her arousal, her slender body bowing beneath him as she tipped back her head and moaned in pleasure.

"Faster," she choked out, her voice harsh as her climax neared.

Rage used his free hand to grasp her hair, turning her face so he could kiss her with savage pleasure at the same time he pumped into her with an insistent rhythm.

"Whatever you desire, Lucie," he swore against her lips.

He plunged his tongue into her mouth, their bodies moving together with a perfect tempo. Then, with a burst of relief, he felt Lucie stiffen, her sharp cry of release echoing through the room.

Rage hissed as her climax gripped his cock, his hips pistoning as he at last gave into the wild hunger of his cat. He gave a shout of satisfaction as his orgasm exploded through him, a tidal wave of rapture rippling through his body.

\* \* \* \*

Lucie collapsed on the bed, too sated to protest when Rage stretched out beside her and possessively tugged her into his arms.

Okay. That'd been…

Stunning. Beautiful. Life altering.

And overall, terrifying.

She liked her sex straightforward and uncomplicated. No weird emotional attachments or expectations. But even as a voice in the back of her mind was urging her to panic, her body was happily snuggling against his hard body, her cat purring in utter contentment.

She would panic later, she promised herself.

After Rage had left her to return to his home.

Lost in her thoughts, Lucie didn't realize that Rage had lifted his head to study her with a brooding gaze. Not until he broke the thick silence.

"Why did you steal my diary?"

Lucie blinked. Wow. That was not at all what she'd been expecting.

She didn't want to talk about the childish stunt. Not because it'd been embarrassing for him. He'd only become more popular with the females after they'd decided his private musings about his lovers somehow enhanced their reputations as desirable mates. Idiots. But because it revealed how desperately obsessed she'd been.

And still was, for that matter.

Acutely aware of his deepening curiosity, she forced herself to shrug. "I was a brat," she said in light tones.

"No." His fingers brushed through her hair, his touch achingly tender. "You were hurt and striking out. I'm just not sure why I was singled out for public humiliation."

"Because…" The words stuck in her throat.

"Lucie?"

She heaved a resigned sigh. He wasn't going to let it go. Not until he coerced her into revealing the painful truth.

"Because I had a crush on you," she grudgingly muttered.

The violet eyes shimmered with flecks of gold as the dawning sun splashed through the windows.

"A crush?"

She grimaced. She might as well confess the rest. If she were being honest, she probably owed him.

"Don't act surprised. You had to sense that I watched you from the trees."

"I thought you were plotting my death."

"I was young and impressionable, and I was fascinated." Her gaze ran over his lean, perfect features. "You were so gorgeous."

"True." He grunted as she elbowed him in the gut. "Ow."

"But it was more than that," she finished her confession. "You had a…kindness that I desperately wanted for myself."

His teasing expression melted to one of regret, his fingers sliding over the curve of her shoulder.

"I would happily have been kind to you if you hadn't bolted whenever I got near you," he murmured.

She believed him. Rage might have been spoiled, but he'd never been deliberately cruel. His nature was to protect the weak and vulnerable.

"I didn't know how to tell you," she admitted with a wry smile. "So instead I struck out."

His fingers drifted down her collarbone, his enticing musk scenting the air. "From now on, I have a better way for you to express your feelings for me."

She instantly stiffened. It was one thing to confess her feelings when she'd been an idiotic youth. There was no way she was going to share the fact he'd never left her dreams.

"Who said I still have feelings for you?" she belligerently demanded, ignoring the fact that she was lying naked in his arms. "That was a long time ago."

He chuckled, not fooled for a second. Damn him.

"Fine, then I'll show you how I feel," he murmured, lowering his head to brand a path of tiny kisses over her brow and down the length of her nose. Then, at last reaching her mouth, he nibbled at her bottom lip. "In fact, I intend to show you how I feel several times a night for a very, very long time to come."

His words were no doubt the empty promises he made to every woman. We'll be together forever, blah, blah, blah.

But they didn't feel empty.

They felt like a pledge that resonated deep in her heart.

Instinctively, she lifted her hands to press them against his chest. "Rage."

He raised his head, staring down at her with a fierce determination. "Do I frighten you?"

"Yes," she admitted without hesitation. "This is all happening too fast."

She caught a glimpse of his cat lurking in his eyes…hungry, possessive. Then, with a visible effort, he gained command of his animal.

A rueful smile touched his lips. "I know."

"I need to check the trace." Lucie muttered a curse, slipping out of bed and heading into the shower.

A charming Rage was as lethal as a possessive Rage.

Twenty minutes later she was scrubbed clean, with her hair braided and wearing her usual uniform of jeans and a long-sleeved T-shirt. Adding a pair of jogging shoes, she returned to the bedroom to discover that Rage had used the guest shower and was already dressed and waiting for her.

His beautiful face was carefully bland as he folded his arms over his chest. Smart male. The intimacy of the night had left her feeling raw and unnervingly vulnerable. One smartass comment and she would have him tossed out of her house.

Without a word, she left the bedroom and headed back to her hidden computer office. Acutely aware of the male prowling a few inches behind her, she slid into her chair and forced herself to concentrate on the computer screen that was blinking with success.

"I have a hit," she murmured, resisting the urge to give her trusty computer a pat.

Not everyone understood her habit of treating her equipment like they were old friends.

Leaning over her shoulder, Rage surrounded her in his warm, male musk. "You found the bastard?"

"I located the computer that is running the auction," she cautioned. "Whether or not the person who's ultimately responsible for setting it up is physically there…" She shrugged. "That's impossible to say."

He nodded. "Where is the computer?"

"Bossier City."

"Damn." Rage abruptly straightened, pacing from one end to the other of the long, narrow room. "That's where Locke was setting up the military lab."

Lucie grimaced, easily understanding his frustration. Stanton Locke had been the human who'd been experimenting with Pantera blood and intending to share it with a military contractor. If the computer was in the same spot, it couldn't be a coincidence.

"So the mystery man might actually have the research notes." She spoke his fears out loud.

"Yep," he growled.

Lucie hit a button on the keypad, then reached to the side as the printer spit out a paper with the information she'd located. Rising to her feet, she handed the printout to Rage.

"Here's the address."

Folding the paper, he shoved it in the back pocket of his jeans, moving to stand directly in front of her.

"The Pantera is in your debt," he assured her, his fingers lightly tracing her jaw.

A tiny shiver raced through her. God. She loved the heat of his touch. It felt as if she'd been branded. Claimed.

*So dangerous…*

"I'll come up with a payment plan," she muttered.

Without warning, he leaned to press a light kiss to her lips. "I have to deal with this, but I swear I'll be back."

Lucie stepped back, her brows lifting in surprise at his words.

Did he think that she was just going to sit home like a good little girl while he had all the fun?

"I'm coming with you."

Rage stiffened, his eyes narrowing. "No way."

She folded her arms over her chest, not for the first time wishing she wasn't so tiny. It was hard to be intimidating when she was a foot shorter than everyone.

"I wasn't asking permission," she informed him.

"You're a Geek, not a Hunter," he growled.

She rolled her eyes. "I'm aware of that."

He leaned down until they were nose to nose, the power of his cat pulsing through the air.

"You've done your job. Now it's my turn."

Her animal prowled beneath her skin, instinctively wanting to back down beneath the stronger male, but Lucie refused to be intimidated. Not just because she was stubborn and overly independent, but because there was no way in hell she was going to let this male walk into danger alone.

That was unacceptable.

"You need me," she told him, meeting him glare for glare.

Taking advantage of their proximity, he swiped his rough tongue over her bottom lip. Such a cat.

"That's true," he agreed in husky tones. "But first I have to put an end to this threat."

She pulled back, resisting the urge to do a little licking of her own. Later…

"I mean, you need to me to stop the auction," she insisted. "Unless you've become a computer expert?"

His brooding gaze lingered on her lips. "With enough encouragement, I can force the bastard to end it."

She didn't doubt that. For all of Rage's easy charm, he was a ruthless predator who would do whatever was necessary to get the information the Pantera needed.

A knowledge that she intended to use to force him to take her along.

"And if he won't? Or if he manages to escape?" she demanded. "Or you accidentally kill him?" She held up her hand as his lips parted to assure her that he could take care of the enemy. "The auction is set on a timer. It's going to happen unless I can gain physical access to his computer and stop it."

His lips snapped together at her indisputable logic.

They both knew that right now, nothing mattered but halting the sell of the technology that would use Pantera blood as some sort of weapon.

"Dammit." Reaching into his pocket, he yanked out his cellphone. "I need to call Parish."

Knowing she'd won, Lucie turned and headed forward to the door. "I'll wait for you in the garage."

# Chapter 5

Rage completed his call to Parish and then took a few minutes to regain control of his temper.

Damn, Lucie. She was supposed to be in her beautiful home, doing whatever it was she did on her fancy computer system. She wasn't supposed to be directly confronting their enemy and putting herself in danger.

Unfortunately, he couldn't deny her logic.

They knew nothing about the person responsible for setting up the auction. Or even if they were still in Bossier City It was only reasonable to have a backup plan to make sure they could prevent the information from being spread to some unknown buyer.

Once he'd managed to gain command of his anger, he followed the scent of primroses to the narrow flight of stairs that led to the garage. Entering the small space, his brows lifted at the sight of the Harley-Davidson Sportster motorcycle.

It was a sleek, fast work of art.

Just like his Lucie.

"Why am I not surprised?" he murmured.

Tossing him a helmet, she tugged on her own before she straddled the bike and started the engine with a throaty roar.

"Get on," she commanded.

Rage put on his helmet. It wasn't that he was afraid of an accident. Pantera could take one hell of a beating. But they didn't have time to be stopped by the local police.

Crossing the floor, he studied the female who was impatiently waiting to leave. "Why can't I drive?"

She sent him a wry glance. "You got to drive in bed."

Heat streaked through him at the vivid memory of her bent in front of him as he took her from behind. Instantly, he was hard.

"True," he murmured.

She flipped down her visor, revving the engine. "Are you coming or not?"

Swinging his leg over the bike, he settled in close behind her, wrapping his arms tightly around her waist.

"This gives me ideas," he said, rubbing his erection against her lower back.

"Stop that," she chided, trying to pretend her arousal wasn't scenting the air. They just had to be in the same room for desire to combust between them.

She pressed a small device that was mounted on the front of the bike, opening the narrow door of the garage, then gunning the engine, they shot onto the narrow side street that was thankfully empty at the early hour.

Rage gave a low chuckle. If he couldn't keep Lucie tucked safely at home, then he was going to enjoy their time together.

Keeping his chin planted against her shoulder, he held on tight as they headed out of New Orleans. The morning air was edged with a sharp chill as they hit the highway and headed north, but neither noticed. Instead, they silently appreciated the close press of their bodies.

Finally, it was Lucie who broke the silence, speaking through the Bluetooth that was built into their helmets.

"What did Parish say?"

Rage grimaced. The leader of the Hunters hadn't been any happier than he was at the thought of Lucie being exposed to their enemy.

"That he would slice off my balls if you got hurt," he admitted, his ears still ringing from the older male's angry warnings. Then, unable to resist his primitive instincts, he asked the question that was gnawing at him. "Are you going to tell me what's up between the two of you?"

"Nothing's up." She easily weaved through the thickening traffic, clearly as at ease on the bike as she was behind her computer. Her skill was oddly erotic. "Parish is my friend."

He believed her. Parish was not only happily mated, but if he'd wanted this female, then nothing on this earth would have kept him from her side.

"Why him?" he demanded.

She snorted. "Because he's a pushy pain in the ass who refuses to take no for an answer."

"That sounds like Parish," he swiftly agreed. "What did he do?"

"He came to me after my grandfather died."

Rage clenched his teeth. Christ, he wished he'd known what her grandfather had been doing. He'd have given the bastard a taste of his own medicine.

"Is that when you burned down the cabin?" he asked.

"Yes." He felt her shiver and he tightened his arms, trying to offer her comfort. It was too late to do any good, but it was all he had. "I had to destroy the memories of that place."

"I don't blame you."

She shrugged. "Maybe someday I'll be able to accept that it was the sickness that made him so cruel, but not yet."

He hoped she did find some peace in the memory of her grandfather. Bitterness would only eat away at her soul.

"Did Parish help you leave the Wildlands?" he inquired.

She nodded. "Once Xavier told me that I was no longer allowed to work on the computers, he offered me an apartment and gave me some money. I think he was afraid I might do something crazy."

Rage gave a short laugh. Like she hadn't been doing crazy shit before then?

Of course, he wasn't stupid enough to point out her habit of striking out without warning.

"I'm glad that Parish was there for you," he said instead, ignoring his cat's growl in protest.

His animal might be convinced that he was the one who was supposed to protect her, but at the time he hadn't given her what she needed. Thank the goddess, Parish had.

He shook off his cat's urge to pout. He hadn't taken care of Lucie in the past, but he fully intended to be the only one to see to her needs in the future.

"You know that Xavier's going to do everything in his power to get you back after this?" he warned.

She buzzed around a truck pulling a wagon of hay. "There's nothing he could offer that would tempt me to return," she proclaimed. "I like my life."

He pressed his hand flat against her stomach, his touch deliberately possessive. He was willing to spend part of their time in New Orleans if that made her happy, but he intended to make sure that she shared his home in the bayous.

"He's not going to be the only one trying to convince you to return to the Wildlands."

"Whatever you say."

Rage frowned at her flippant words, turning them over in his head. There was some sort of message in them. He knew women well enough to realize that there were always hidden meanings when a woman was acting as if it didn't matter. A smart male learned to decipher them.

It took several minutes, then, like a bolt of lightning, it hit him.

Hell. She'd decided he was a frivolous flirt. A male who drifted from one bed to another. And right now, there was nothing he could say that was going to make her believe that he wanted more than a casual affair. Obviously he was going to have to prove his sincerity with deeds.

A grim smile of determination curved his lips. "You can doubt me, Lucie, but eventually you'll accept you're not getting rid of me."

"That sounds like a threat," she muttered.

His fingers skimmed up until they were just an inch from the delicate curve of her breast. "A promise."

She shivered, reaching up to turn off her Bluetooth. Rage smiled. She could try to shut him out as much as she wanted.

Nothing, not even her stubborn distrust, was going to stop him from claiming her as his own.

\* \* \* \*

Lucie pretended an all-consuming concentration on navigating the five-and-a-half-hour drive to Bossier City. Not that she was stupid enough to think for a second that she was fooling Rage. They both knew that she'd have to be dead not to be aware of the six-foot plus male who was snuggled so tightly against her back she could feel every inch of his hard body. That didn't even include the sparks of awareness that were sizzling between them. She wouldn't be surprised if her skin was scorched from the heat.

Thankfully, she managed to arrive at their destination without crashing. Or halting the bike so she could rip off Rage's clothes and have her evil way with him, which had been way more likely than crashing.

Pulling the bike to a halt a block away, she nodded her head toward the large warehouse that overlooked the Red River.

"That's the place."

Rage stepped off the bike and removed his helmet, his gaze locked on the brick structure that looked abandoned from a distance. Lucie, however, didn't miss the new chain link fence that was ten-foot tall and topped with barbed wire. Or the bars that'd recently been added to the windows. Someone didn't want any stray trespassers having a peek inside.

"Stay here while I check it out," he murmured.

Lucie reached out to lay her hand on his arm. Shit. She didn't want him going in there alone.

"I should come with you."

He shoved back his hair with impatient fingers, clearly anxious to be on the hunt.

"You're staying here."

"But—"

"When it comes to geeky stuff, you're in charge," he interrupted, tugging off her helmet so he could stare down at her with a ruthless air of authority.

The casual charmer was replaced with the lethal predator.

"Geeky stuff?"

"When it comes to hunting the enemy, I'm in charge." He reached to cup her chin in his hand, forcing her to meet his steady gaze. "Deal?"

Lucie hesitated. Once she agreed, she would be giving her word that she would be stuck waiting for him, even if her every instinct screamed she should be with him. What if he went in and never came out? What if she truly lost him?

The thought made her heart clench with panic.

Unfortunately, she knew that he wasn't going to leave until he had her promise.

Stubborn cat.

"Deal," she grudgingly conceded.

Easily sensing how difficult it'd been for her to accept his demand, Rage leaned down to brush his lips lightly over her mouth.

"I'll come and get you once I'm sure it's safe."

She reached up to grasp his sweatshirt, a strange sense of premonition inching down her spine.

"Be careful."

"Always."

He paused long enough to steal one last lingering kiss before he was straightening and jogging down the street, staying in the shadows of the nearby buildings. She held her breath as he reached the fence and scaled it with fluid ease. He was fast, but they didn't know anything about the enemy's security.

No alarms sounded as he jogged across the empty parking lot and entered through a back window, but Lucie knew that didn't mean anything.

Crawling off the bike, Lucie stored the helmets before she pulled out her phone. She wanted to call Parish and ask the leader of the Hunters what Rage had said to him earlier. And more importantly, she wanted to make sure he was sending backup in case things went to hell.

She frowned as she scrolled through her contacts, feeling an odd prickle in the center of her back.

It felt as if she was being stalked.

The thought had barely formed when she caught the unmistakable scent of a human male. Glancing up, she watched as a man jumped from a second floor window to land directly in front her. The stranger was dressed in camo pants and a green henley that was stretched tight over his bulging muscles. His face was square with blunt features, and his dirty blond hair was pulled into a short tail at his neck.

Lucie grimaced. Damn. She didn't need the edge of musk that clung to the man's body to realize he'd been drinking Pantera blood. That leap would have broken the legs of an average human.

Shoving her phone back into her pocket, she pinned a faux smile to her lips. The man might have juiced himself on Pantera blood, but that didn't make him any match for the real deal.

"Nice trick, stud," she murmured as she strolled forward. A few more feet and she would be in striking distance. "I was just waiting for my boyfriend, but the jerk is late. Again. Maybe we should—"

"Don't move, bitch," the man snapped, reaching into a holster to pull out…was that a dart gun?

She narrowed her gaze. "You have no idea what kind of bitch I can be," she growled.

He pointed the gun at the center of her chest. "Hands behind your back."

Yeah, right. Like she was going to give him an opportunity to cuff her with those zip-locks she could see dangling from his belt.

"Fuck off," she snarled, surging forward.

She'd managed to get her fingers wrapped around his thick neck when he squeezed the trigger and she was hit by a small dart. Instantly, a crippling pain exploded through her.

It wasn't the tranq gun she'd assumed.

Instead, the dart was filled with malachite, the one thing that could decapitate a Pantera. The mineral not only hurt like hell, but it cut her connection to her cat, leaving her as helpless as an injured human.

Shit, shit, shit.

Nearly paralyzed by the poison pumping through her blood, Lucie didn't even put up a fight when the man grabbed her by the waist and tossed her over his shoulder.

"Bad little kitty," he mocked, smacking his hand on her ass. "I have ways of punishing you."

Her head bounced against his back as he headed down the street and through a narrow gate in the chain link fence. Lucie gave a low groan. They were going to the warehouse where Rage had so recently disappeared. She could only hope that he was well hidden.

Entering the building through a side door, the man carried her up a set of metal stairs to the loft on the fourth floor.

"I got her," her captor called out.

Lucie caught the scent of two more males, both humans who'd used Pantera blood to enhance their power.

"Put her in the cell," one of the males commanded.

There was the sound of the man's heavy boots hitting the wood plank floor as she was carried across the room and roughly dumped into a cage made of iron bars that was shoved against the wall. She hit the ground with a bone-jarring thud, glaring at the man who slammed the door shut and locked it.

He ignored her seething fury, turning on his heel to head toward the two men who were standing beside a long folding table that was loaded with various computer and surveillance equipment.

It was obviously a temporary setup. The numerous cords were hanging from the rafters, the monitors were resting on cheap TV trays, and the only places to sit were plastic patio chairs. Once the auction was done, they intended to pack up shop and get the hell out of Dodge. Or Bossier City.

Despite her pain, her heart skipped a beat.

This was exactly what they'd come here to find.

If she could get out of the cage, she could...

Her thoughts were brought to a sharp end as one of the men strolled toward the cage, eyeing her with a vulgar heat that made her skin crawl.

"She's a pretty little thing," he drawled, his narrow face and thin frame reminding Lucie of a rat. "I think I might have a taste of her."

Lucie tensed, cursing the malachite that continued to cripple her. She wasn't sure if she could fight off the jerk or not.

"You can have fun with her later," the oldest of the men thankfully snapped, pointing toward one of the monitors. "First we need her to capture our unwelcomed visitor."

Lucie made a strangled sound as she crawled to the edge of the cage to catch the image in the monitor.

Rage.

Oh, hell. They knew he was in the building. And they were going to use her to try and capture him.

On cue, the older man, who was clearly the leader of the trio, reached to touch a button on a silver panel arranged in the center of the table.

"Pantera, we know you're here," he said into and old-fashion microphone, the words echoing through the warehouse. "Move to the doorway and go to your knees with your hands behind your head until my guard can arrive."

Lucie watched the monitor as Rage came to a startled halt, his gaze lifting toward the ceiling of the room he was standing in before he was flipping off the camera pointed directly at him.

"Now, now, that's not very nice," the human continued, his tone taunting. "You should be more grateful. After all, we have your pretty companion all safely tucked in her cage waiting for you. It was so rude of you to leave her waiting on the street. Anyone could have come along and hurt her."

Rage's eyes filled with the golden fury of his cat. He couldn't shift away from the Wildlands, but his animal gave him a speed and strength that no human could match. Which was obviously why they'd taken Lucie as their hostage.

Silently praying that the Hunter would be smart enough to escape and wait for backup, Lucie's stomach twisted with dread as he slowly lifted his hands in surrender.

"No, Rage," she screamed. "Get out."

The man standing near the cage reached through the bars to smash his fist into her face, the blow violent enough to snap her nose. She felt the rush of blood as she tumbled to the side, smacking her head on the floor. Weakened by the malachite, she couldn't battle back the darkness that rushed up to claim her.

Her last thought was that she'd never, ever had anyone sacrifice themselves for her...

# Chapter 6

Lying in the center of the cage, Rage pressed his body against the unconscious Lucie, silently contemplating the various ways he intended to kill his captors.

Ripping out their throats was always the easiest. But there was a certain satisfaction in the thought of slowly peeling off their skin. Or maybe he'd wait and let Lucie decide how she wanted them to die.

That seemed fair considering they'd broken her nose.

A low growl rumbled in his throat. Even though she'd healed over the past few hours, he was never going to forget his first sight of her crumpled in a heap with blood pouring down her face. If he hadn't been able to pick up the steady beat of her heart, he might very well have torn apart the three humans with his bare hands.

Instead, he'd allowed the men to shove him into the cell. Idiots. It was exactly where he wanted to be.

He'd known from the second he'd heard the human's voice over the intercom that he was going to have to change his plans. It was no longer a matter of finding the mystery man and forcing him to halt the auction. He had to get to Lucie.

End of story.

Thankfully, he'd managed to make a quick call to Parish before the guard arrived. He'd asked for the backup Pantera that were on their way to the warehouse to stay hidden in the neighborhood until he had Lucie away from the humans.

She was, he'd swiftly determined, their only hope to stop the auction.

His little time with the leader of the trio had already convinced him that the bastard wasn't going to give up his shot at a fortune. The human had clearly sacrificed everything to join Benson Enterprises. His reputation as a legitimate researcher, his place in the academic world, and his morals. Now that it was collapsing around him, he was obsessed with getting what he'd been promised.

Money. And a lot of it.

Parish had given him until eleven p.m. to escape with his soon-to-be mate. Then the Hunters were coming in. Which meant that they had less than an hour for Lucie to wake up before the cavalry came charging in and they lost this last opportunity.

Burying his face in her hair, he breathed deep of her primrose scent, his cat pressing against his skin as it tried to comfort his female. Then, without warning, he felt her stir in his arms.

"Rage?" she murmured in a husky voice.

Sitting up, he carefully scooped her in his arms so he could cradle her in his lap. "I've got you, sweetheart."

She blinked in confusion, her face still pale from the malachite that had ravaged her body. Although the poison had worked its way out of her system, she would be weak for hours.

"Where are we…" Her words trailed away as she realized they were sitting in the middle of a cage.

Then, astonishingly, she wiggled until she could free her arm to punch him in the center of his chest.

Rage scowled. Not because it hurt. Even at full strength she couldn't do much damage. She was a Geek, not a Hunter. But in sheer surprise.

Perhaps he was crazy, but he'd expected some gratitude that he'd come to save her.

Just a smidgeon.

"What was that for?" he demanded.

She scowled right back at him. "What the hell is wrong with you?"

"My mother would tell you nothing," he assured her. "As far as she's concerned, I'm perfect."

She rolled her eyes, not nearly as impressed as she should have been.

"If you were perfect then you wouldn't have been stupid enough to surrender to the enemy."

He shrugged. "You needed me."

"That's not the point." She gave him another punch, but Rage didn't miss the hint of vulnerability that softened her features. She'd never had anyone who truly cared about her. She didn't know how to deal with his concern. "It's your duty to escape so you could stop the research from being sold."

He grabbed her face in his hands, staring down at her with a grim intensity.

"I couldn't risk you," he growled. "Nothing is more important to me than your safety." He tilted his head down until they were nose to nose. "I will sacrifice everything, including my duty, to protect you."

Their gazes locked, the weight of his words vibrating in the air.

It was a pledge not even Lucie could dismiss as his usual flirtations.

She licked her lips, a rapid pulse fluttering at the base of her throat. "You are…"

"What?" he prompted as her words faded away.

The emotions she usually kept so rigidly contained slowly darkened her eyes. Need, hope, and something that Rage desperately wanted to believe was love.

"Impossible," she at last muttered, reaching up to tangle her fingers in his hair as she planted a possessive kiss on his lips.

Pleasure exploded through him.

It was the first time she'd initiated a kiss. It made the caress all the more sweet.

Stroking his fingers down the slender arch of her throat, he savored the feel of her lips as they demanded his response. Deep inside, his cat purred with contentment, even as it twitched with the need to get his female out of this cage and back to the safety of the Wildlands.

Lifting his head, he gazed down at her with a faint smile. "Obviously you're dangerously addicted to males who are impossible," he teased.

She rolled her eyes, but even as her lips parted to punish him for his smartass comment, she was sucking in a sharp breath.

"Shit, what time is it?"

Rage reached down to pull out the cell phone he'd hidden beneath his sweatshirt. The idiots hadn't bothered to frisk him before throwing him in the cage.

"Just after ten."

Scrambling off his lap, Lucie shakily rose to her feet to glance around the empty loft.

"Where are the humans?"

Rage shoved himself upright to stand next to his female. She was too stubborn to lean on him, but he'd make damned sure he was close enough to catch her if she fell.

"The leader just stepped out of the room," he told her, nodding toward the door across the room. "The other two are keeping watch on the lower floor. They seem to think there might be other Pantera on the way."

She arched her brows. "Are there?"

He leaned down to speak directly in her ear. He couldn't be sure they weren't being monitored by a hidden camera.

"They're waiting for my signal."

Following his lead, she kept her voice soft enough that it wouldn't carry. "Then why haven't you signaled?"

"I needed you awake so you can stop the auction."

She blinked, as if caught off guard that he'd managed to fight his natural instincts to ensure she was rescued as swiftly as possible. It spoke of his absolute faith in her. Not only as a computer whiz. But as a loyal Pantera who was willing to take risks to protect her pack.

Reaching out, she placed a hand in the center of his chest, a soul-deep gratitude etched on her pale face.

"Actually, I can do better than that," she promised, glancing toward the door of their cell. "But in case you didn't notice, we're locked in a cage."

"I can take care of the cage." He laid his hand over hers, pressing it tight against the steady beat of his heart. "Are you feeling up to doing your thing?"

A slow, wicked smile of anticipation curved her lips. "Yeah, I think I can manage my thing. What about the humans?"

"They're my thing," he assured her. Lifting her hand, he pressed his lips to the center of her palm. "Ready?"

She lifted herself on her tiptoes to place a fleeting kiss on his lips before she was stepping back with a determined expression.

"Ready," she said, clearly expecting him to do something "James Bond" like pick the lock or discover some hidden lever that would open the door. Instead, he moved forward to grab the iron bars, and with one massive burst of strength, ripped the door off its hinges. "Shit, Rage," she breathed in shock.

He pointed toward the computer. The humans might have limited hearing, but even they couldn't have missed the screech of metal. They'd have only seconds before their captors were rushing to the loft.

"You concentrate on making sure that intel doesn't get out. I'll make sure you're not interrupted."

He turned to head toward the door, only to halt when she reached out to grasp his arm.

"Rage..." Her words trailed away, as if she couldn't force them past a lump in her throat.

"I know," he murmured softly, leaning down to press a tender kiss against her forehead. "I'll be back for you, Lucie. I swear."

Not giving himself the opportunity to waver from his decision to leave her alone to work her magic with the computers, he jogged across the wooden planks and slipped out the door. Then, holding onto the steel handle, he gave it a violent twist, jamming the lock so no one would be able to open the door if something happened to him.

At least...no human would be able to open it.

A Pantera would be able to get into the loft and rescue Lucie if necessary.

Pausing to take a thorough survey of his surroundings, Rage at last moved to the bottom of the metal steps. The door was the only entry to the upper floor. As long as he could block the stairs, no one was going to get to Lucie.

He had less than a second to glance around the large, open storage room before a shadowed form was entering through an open doorway, quickly followed by one of the guards.

"What the hell..." The leader of the humans came to an abrupt halt as he caught sight of Rage in the faint moonlight that spilled in from a small window. "How did you get out?"

"Did you really think that flimsy cage was going to halt a full-blooded Pantera?" he taunted, folding his arms over his chest with a nonchalance that he hoped would unnerve his prey.

The older man scowled, glancing around the room. "Where's the woman?"

Rage shrugged. "She already escaped."

The goon standing behind the leader turned back toward the doorway. "I'll get her."

"Don't be an idiot," the leader snapped, pointing toward the stairs. "She's still upstairs. We have to stop her before she can disrupt the auction."

The goon frowned. Clearly he'd been hired for his oversized muscles, not his intelligence.

"You said it couldn't be stopped once it started."

"Not unless someone gains access to my computer," the leader snarled. "I have to get up there."

The goon nodded, grimly glancing toward Rage, who flashed a wide grin.

"I don't doubt you have limited brain power, human, but do you really think you can take on a full-blooded Pantera?"

The man narrowed his gaze, stepping forward. "I'm not afraid of you, beast-man."

Rage resisted the urge to roll his eyes. Beast-man?

Whatever.

"It's your funeral," he said, his lips twisting into a humorless smile as the goon fumbled for the gun he'd shoved into the waistband of his jeans.

Sloppy.

The tight material meant that he couldn't draw his weapon cleanly. It was all the opening that Rage needed.

With a low growl, he leaped forward, grabbing the man by the neck. His fingers sank into the thick muscles, lifting the heavy body off the ground. Reaching down, he grabbed the weapon and tossed it into the corner. He didn't want to attract any more guards with the sound of gunfire.

Distantly, he was aware of the older man rushing toward the stairs, but he wasn't foolish enough to allow his attention to stray from the man who was struggling to get free of Rage's iron grip. The goon might be human, but he'd been injected with Pantera blood, which meant he was faster, stronger, and possessed more endurance than a normal person.

Squeezing even tighter, he grimly shoved the man against the wall, trying to avoid the kicks that were aimed at his knees. Was the bastard half mule? At the same time, he was forced to dodge the massive fists that were aimed at his face.

His grip, however, never faltered.

The man grunted, his face turning a strange shade of puce as his eyes slowly glazed over. Still, it was several minutes later before the large body at last went limp and Rage allowed him to drop to the floor. Then, just to make sure that the goon wasn't faking, he stepped forward and kicked him in the face with enough force the make his head slam back against the wall.

Okay, it wasn't just to ensure he was truly unconscious.

He wanted the bastard to pay for hurting Lucie.

For now a busted nose, split lip, and concussion would have to do.

Confident the man wasn't going to be moving for several hours, Rage paused to suck in a deep breath. He could smell the other human guard two floors down, no doubt watching the entrance.

Which meant he only had to worry about the man who had climbed the stairs and was currently pounding on the door of the loft, as if that would magically make it open.

Climbing the steps in two long leaps, he watched in satisfaction as the human turned to stare at him in blatant horror. It was always nice when his prey had the opportunity to regret making an enemy of the Pantera.

Licking his lips, the leader pressed his back against the door and lifted his hands in a pleading gesture.

"Look, there's no reason we can't work together," the man said, beads of sweat trickling down his thin face. "There's going to be plenty of money to share."

Rage curled his upper lip in disgust. "You think I would betray my people for money?"

"What do you want? Women? Power?"

A growl rumbled in Rage's chest. "Your head mounted on my wall."

The man shook his head. "There has to be something—"

His words broke off as the door was suddenly wrenched open from inside to reveal Lucie. She flashed a smile as she caught sight of Rage and the trembling human.

"It's done," she said with blatant satisfaction.

"Done?" The man paled as he glanced over Lucie's shoulders to his table of computer equipment.

Rage didn't bother asking technical questions. It wasn't like he was going to understand Geek-speak. If Lucie said it was done…it was done.

As simple as that.

Which meant it was time for him to complete his job.

Reaching out, he grabbed the man by the material of his designer shirt, roughly hauling him down the steps and out of the storage room.

"No." The human squirmed, futilely attempting to dig in his heels, and Rage hauled him across the floor to the long bank of windows that overlooked the river. "We can make a deal," he rasped. "Just tell me your price."

"My price?" With a quick motion, Rage had the man lifted off his feet and with one brutal movement, he was shoving him through the nearest window. "This is my price."

There was the sound of glass shattering and a shrill scream as the man flew out the window and down to the parking lot below. He landed with a sickening thud.

Moving forward, Rage studied the limp form that was spread eagle on the pavement, his lips twitching as he watched the second guard dash out of the building to take in the sight of his dead leader. The guard glanced up to catch sight of Rage, his face draining of color before he was ducking his head and running away like a true coward.

Rage shook his head. The Pantera that surrounded the area would catch the idiot before he managed to escape.

Which meant that his job was done. At least for now.

Stepping away from the window, he turned to discover Lucie standing just a few feet away, studying him with a faint smile.

"Happy now?"

"Not yet," he admitted, prowling forward to wrap his arms tightly around her slender curves. Instantly his cat purred in approval, savoring the knowledge his female was safe and exactly where she needed to be. Tucked against his body. Planting a kiss on the top of her head, he sucked in a deep breath of her primrose scent. "But I intend to take you back to the Wildlands and get very, very happy."

# Epilogue

Rage watched his female with a growing sense of frustration.

Okay, he was delighted to see her surrounded by a crowd of admiring Geeks as she explained exactly how she'd managed to destroy over a hundred computer systems, expose two terrorist cells to Homeland Security, and nearly topple the dictator of a small country.

She deserved every single pat on the back, not to mention more than one apology for not reaching out to her years ago.

But, enough was enough.

This was *his* female.

He wanted some up close and personal time.

No doubt sensing he was on the edge of shoving his way through the crowd that filled the long meeting room on the top floor of the Diplomats headquarters, Parish moved to stand at his side, placing a restraining hand on his shoulder.

"She's a hero," the leader of the Hunter's softly murmured.

"Yep," Rage readily agreed, his heart swelling with pride. "It was a brilliant idea to booby-trap the payload."

While Rage had been dealing with the humans, his genius mate had been layering the files that were being auctioned with a hidden code. It was the sort of snare only a hacker could have created.

"And even more brilliant to make sure that they were all chosen as the highest bidder. Every asshole involved in the auction was hit with the nasty virus that created a backdoor that Xavier could use to download the information from the computers involved before wiping their hard drives."

Rage chuckled. "Xavier said that the howls of pain were epic across the Internet."

"And most blame Benson Enterprises," Parish said, soul-deep pleasure shimmering in his golden eyes. They were all celebrating the chance to strike such a decisive blow against their enemies. "It will be a while before Christopher recovers from this latest catastrophe."

Rage grimaced. None of them would be safe until they managed to track down the mysterious leader of Benson Enterprises and put an end to him.

Thankfully, that was someone else's problem. For tonight, Rage intended to devote himself to his beautiful mate.

First, however, there was a question that had been nagging at him.

"Are you going to tell me why you sent me to find Lucie instead of going yourself?" he demanded of his companion.

Parish smiled. "Because I knew that Lucie was always fascinated by you." The older man rolled his eyes. "The goddess knows why. But since she is more deserving of happiness than anyone else I know, I thought I would try my hand at playing cupid."

Rage narrowed his gaze. "So you set me up?"

"Absolutely."

Rage abruptly wrapped his arms around the large man and gave him a hug. "I owe you one, my man."

"Stop that." Parish shoved him away, a gleam of satisfaction in his eyes. "And don't think I won't collect your debt."

"Later." Squaring his shoulders, Rage prepared himself to battle his way to his mate's side. "I have a long overdue date with my female."

*The End*

# Killian

# Chapter 1

Nostrils flared, green eyes narrowed, Rosalie sprinted across the clearing toward the border. Overhead, the quarter moon was barely visible behind a wash of gray clouds.

A storm was coming.

From above.

And from below.

Rosalie's cat grinned with feral menace as she slowed just enough to weave in and out of a trio of massive cypress. Most of the Pantera either feared the truth of the latter—humans invading the Wildlands—or hoped the threat would just go away and the Pantera would be left in peace once again. Hidden once again. But not Rosalie and her cat. They were looking—hoping—for bloodshed.

Human bloodshed.

Thunder growled around her, fueling her desire. Every night now she'd taken to prowling these lands, the border. From dusk to sunrise. Alone. Granted, she never started off alone. That wasn't the Hunter way. Normally, she was put in a group of three. But inevitably, conveniently, she lost them. Ditched them. Most of the other Hunters liked to patrol in their two-legged form; talking, discussing what they'd done that day as well as the strategy for the night's watch. Rosalie wasn't interested in chitchat, planning, or donning her female form. She preferred a solo hunt these days and the protective layer of her puma. Her cat preferred it too. Its heart was heavy and needy.

Pain.

Loss.

*Mercier.*

The puma's belly contracted with the thought of the massive gold cat, and the broad, sable-eyed male who'd been her lover and friend and…savior. Were they looking down at her, watching her? Cat and male. Two separate entities in the beyond. Did they miss her as she missed them?

Night consumed the sky above now, its inky blackness interrupted only by a fissure of diamond-colored lightning every now and again. Rosalie's ears pricked up, catching the cries of Bayon and Jazz about a quarter mile off. Near the east border. They were looking for her. Probably worried about her. All the Hunters seemed to be, even though she'd assured them she was fine. That she'd forgiven Hiss, the Hunter male who'd indirectly brought on Mercier's death. That she'd moved on. They didn't believe her lies. Oh, that ever-present expression of concern on their faces. It was irritating as hell. Parish had even gone so far as to insist she take time off. Said that dealing with both her mate's death and the trauma of the abduction that had nearly claimed her life too, was vital to her sanity and productivity.

But Rosalie didn't do time off.

She was in.

Always in.

Even more so as the war between the humans and the Pantera gained ground. And intensity.

The scent of her kind rushed her nostrils as she neared the bayou. She opened her mouth and inhaled deeply. Not Bayon and Jazz. Nor any Hunter she knew. A whisper of unease moved through her as the sound of splashing lured her closer. Who would be swimming at this hour? Two Pantera…lovers, perhaps? Her lip curled. That's all she needed tonight. *Foolish, unthinking cats. Playing in the water while the enemy lurks right outside our borders.*

And sometimes inside them as well.

She'd give them a stern talking-to. Or her claws would.

She stalked through the thick foliage, ready to pounce, to scare the shit out of some Geeks or Suits or Healers. But she only found one female Healer. And something else entirely.

In that moment, Rosalie ceased to exist, and her cat took full control, an event that was happening a lot lately.

"Fuck, woman," a deep male voice barked from the sleepy waters of the bayou. "I don't want to hurt you."

Eyes narrowed, nostrils flared, ears pricked, Rosalie's cat remained behind a moss-coated cypress. She wanted to spring. Attack. Without even knowing what was happening. She didn't care. No. The cat didn't care.

It scented human.

"You can't come here," a female cried out.

No. Not a female, Rosalie puma's confirmed. Not a woman, either. One of the rescued lab rats who had come to stay in the Wildlands. Something halfway between Pantera and human. Rosalie narrowed her eyes on the female figure in the water. She worked with the Healers. Karen...that was her name. She deserved claws and fangs herself for even engaging with this enemy.

A low, feral growl rumbled in Rosalie's throat. Maybe the male wasn't an enemy to *Karen*. Was this a meeting of lovers? Did the rat have a human male lover?

"Stop!" Karen called as the male swam away from her, toward the shore. "You'll be killed the second you step foot onto the Wildlands."

Rosalie's puma grinned. *Or maybe even before that.*

Her cat leapt from the flora and raced to the shore. The second the dark-haired male was out of the water, she attacked. Teeth sank into wet T-shirt, and with a growl of fury she dragged him onto the mossy bank.

But he was no fragile human with dead instincts. In seconds, he rolled away and sprang to his feet. Wasting no time, Rosalie's puma leapt onto his chest and sent him stumbling back. Cursing, he pushed her away, then found his footing again. Wet, his T-shirt clinging to his hard muscles, he crouched into a fighting position. Deep blue eyes raging at her, taunting her, his lip curled. He wasn't remotely afraid. He knew how to fight. Had been trained to fight.

Her Pantera heart sank while her cat's boiled.

He knew how to fight a Pantera.

She snarled and once again leapt at him, claws extended. He ducked, then flipped her over his back. Recovery was less than five seconds, and again she attacked. This time he turned to face her and swipe her legs out from under her.

*Fuck you, Human.*

The rat, Karen, was on the shore now, and as thunder boomed and lightning flickered in the sky, she tried desperately to calm the situation. But both Rosalie's puma and the man were oblivious. They were circling each other now, eyes narrowed, nostrils flared.

"I don't want to hurt you, kitty cat," he said, his tone dark and dangerous as his blue eyes hardened. "I just want to see—"

Rosalie didn't let him finish. She sprang forward and took him out at the ankles. This time, the man went down. All six foot three inches of muscle and bone. She wrestled him to his back, then stood over him, pinning him to the cold ground. For a few brief seconds, she stared down at him in the quarter moon's cloudy light. Every part of him was hard, from his mouth to his eyes to his body. He was wet, his short black hair plastered to his head. And scented of sweat and the bayou. Some females might call him...*sexy.*

Rosalie would call him dinner.

"Fucking cats," he growled. Then Rosalie's legs were suddenly thrust apart, hands closed around her throat and she was being rolled onto her back.

Panic flooded through her and she unleashed her claws, tried to reach his flesh. Any bit. Draw blood. But...no. Goddess, no. He was so strong. Shockingly strong.

She tried to turn her head, get her teeth on him, in him...

*Fuck!*

Poised above her, his massive, unyielding body weight pinning her cat down, he stared at her. Intently. Curiously. With those blue shark eyes. "I'll let go, Kitten," he whispered. "If you sheath your claws, close your mouth, and listen to what I have to say."

Hatred threatened to consume her...the puma. A human was not only demanding things from her, but he was imprisoning her. Her nostrils flared. Her puma had never felt such a desire to draw and consume blood. If this bastard thought she would ever allow herself to be imprisoned again, he was an idiot.

"What do you think, Kitten?" he said, his tone low with warning, his hard body digging into the flesh of her cat. "Can you control yourself?"

Rosalie granted him the puma's equivalent of a fuck-you grin, then followed that up with a quick and painful butt to the forehead.

The shock was immediate. The pain, too. He cursed, but his grip on her never wavered. Who the hell was this man? That he could contain her? A deadly beast of a Hunter? That he could suffer the pain she inflicted and not retreat?

And why hadn't she scented him when he was in the bayou with the rat?

*Shit. The rat.* Rosalie glanced around. Gone. Unbelievable. Or maybe not... It had abandoned a Pantera. What did she expect from a hybrid? From something developed in that goddamned lab. Mercier would've ripped this man apart then laughed as he fed on the bastard's heart.

The puma's insides deflated in instant pain. Unfortunately, the emotion caused not only her instincts to slow, but the man to get the upper hand.

He'd pulled some type of thin rope from his back pocket and was binding her puma's wrists. She roared into the cold night air for her fellow Hunters and fought against the rope. But it was too late.

"You give me no choice, Kitten," he said. "You drew first blood. You won't get another chance to touch me."

*Touch you? Oh no, Human. Consume you is what I want. What I'll have the moment you turn your back. Or expose your jugular.*

Granted, it was nearly impossible to cool, calm, or regulate the puma in that moment. It wanted only to struggle, get free, fight. *Kill.* But Rosalie had forced herself inside its brain now, and she knew that none of those things would happen if she continued to thrash and snarl. She pushed deep inside herself, to the cat's heart, trying to urge the puma to stop fighting. But it refused her. It was her alpha now. Had been for weeks. It ran the show, and it wasn't backing down or playing dead. Even to get the upper hand.

As her puma snarled and fought and wriggled against the hard, wet earth, the man pressed on. He was shockingly strong and incredibly fast. In under thirty seconds, he had both her back paws tied together, as well as her front.

Panic sliced through Rosalie as she fought for movement. Being bound, contained. It reminded her...

Tears scratched her throat. *Her* throat this time. Not the puma's.

*No. Stop and remember where you are. The Wildlands. Not in that—*

"Fuck no," the man growled, his eyes searching hers before moving over her puma's face. "I'm not turning into this. Those pieces of shit..."

Pain lanced through her, stealing her breath. Pantera. Puma. What was she? Her eyes clamped shut. *Oh Goddess. Goddess, no, please...* But it was happening anyway. Her fur stood on end and her bones started to ache. Without her consent. A shudder built inside her and she felt her cat's thick skin shrink. Tears pricked her eyes as claws, sharp and protective, drew back into the beginnings of fingers. She gasped for air, a strangled cry into the heavy early winter air.

"Shit," uttered the man.

For several brief seconds, Rosalie lay there, naked, her back to the hard earth, her wrists and ankles still bound. On any other night, she'd be fighting, scrambling to get loose, cursing and snarling at the intruder. Promising him a long, arduous death. But not tonight. Humiliation and pain and grief anchored her body to the ground, stiffened her spine. She was that prisoner of the lab again.

Slowly, she allowed her eyelids to lift. Stunned, confused, almost guilty blue eyes blazed down upon her. They held hers momentarily, then blinked and started to descend. A quick sweep. Down her body, then back up again. Assessing. Almost…professional. And yet Rosalie didn't miss the shards of heat he hadn't been quick enough to hide.

Naked. Female.

She couldn't care less. She had never been a prude. With or without fur, she was Pantera.

As he stared at her, Rosalie took stock of her situation. No longer did those ropes encircle thick puma limbs. On her female wrists and ankles the coils were loose. He hadn't noticed. Her mind revved. *Keep his eyes on yours as you slowly slip from your bindings.*

As she moved a centimeter at a time out of the ropes, she stared at him. She despised the way he looked. How tall he was—all the hard muscle, the close-cropped black hair, and the arrogant, sharp-angled face. But she especially despised those blue eyes. They changed too swiftly. From blank to predatory to thoughtful. As if he had a soul—or worse, a conscience.

Rosalie knew there were humans living in the Wildlands. Good, decent, kind humans. But they were all female. The men…well, every single human man she had ever known was a terror. Unfeeling. Sadistic. Would do anything to get what he wanted no matter who got in the way or who got hurt.

*Like our friend here.*

Ankles and wrists free now, Rosalie held her position. The man was staring at her mouth. Like he was hypnotized. *Fool.* With barely a breath, she attacked. Her knee slammed into his hard stomach just as the heel of her hand thrust up into his chin. A grunt of pain met her ears, but she didn't stop. Squeezing him tight, she rolled hard right, and once he was on his back she dropped down on his chest and wrapped her hands around his neck, her thumbs instantly pressing into his windpipe.

Shock and fury registered first in those blue eyes, then, as his eyes flickered down her body to her breasts and belly and sex, desire blazed.

*Fuck you, Human,* she thought blackly even as her body betrayed her with a wash of sexual awareness. *You don't get this. Me. Ever.*

No longer bound, no longer a prisoner, it was the easiest shift in the world. From Rosalie back to her puma. And the cat ruled. It was alpha. It carried the anger with no grief. It desired blood, not touch or taste or connection. It was the ultimate strength.

With a flourish and a snarl of fury, the cat emerged. Claws dug into thick muscle, and mouth opened to reveal sharp, impressive teeth—ready…so ready.

But just as the puma was about to sink its fangs into the male's neck, it froze. For a voice.

"No, Rosalie."

Master and commander.

Not Parish. That would have her puma slow but not stop. It was Raphael. Leader of the Pantera. And every male and female, no matter what form they took, listened and obeyed.

A growl vibrated in her cat's throat. It didn't want to obey. It wanted vengeance.

"Get off now," Raphael continued in a voice so quietly threatening it buried itself within her.

Rosalie, the female inside the puma, tried to obey. Really. Tried. But it was...

"We have him, Rosalie," Raphael whispered near her ear.

*No. I have him. And I want his blood.*

*Blood for blood.*

The last words she heard were, "Take it," before something pricked the back of her cat's neck and she was being pulled off the human, her strength—that reliable, impenetrable strength—now gone.

# Chapter 2

Propped up on a hospital-type bed, Killian watched as the doctor—or whatever they called them here...Healer?— stitched him up. Three fairly deep puncture wounds on his left shoulder. That damn wildcat.

*That fucking gorgeous wildcat.*

Killian erased the thought from his head immediately. It had no place there. He was in the Wildlands on a mission of survival. Not to entertain attractions. Especially to a creature who'd nearly gutted him like a fish on the bank of the bayou not two hours ago.

Something flickered on inside him and he glanced up. The leader of the Pantera was now in his hospital room, standing next to one of the guards who had been stationed here since Killian was brought in.

*What the fuck?* How had Killian not heard him?

*Shit...*he'd felt him, though...hadn't he?

Killian took a second to assess the man. He looked exactly like his picture. The one in the dossier kept at the lab, that is. Not the ones online or in the newspapers. Those all looked Photoshopped. His features had been softened, making him look less threatening. More approachable, for a mysterious shape shifter from a hidden world called the Wildlands. A declawed cat in an Armani suit. But the truth of it was that this guy was as deadly as the Glock Killian had lost at the bottom of the bayou a couple of hours ago. Maybe even more so.

"So," Raphael started, looking up. His gold eyes were reserved. "Tell me, Killian O'Roarke. Why has a member of the United States military crossed the border into the Wildlands and demanded to see me?"

A muscle flickered in Killian's jaw as he held the man's stare. The only information he'd given the Healer working on him was his first name. "Don't know any O'Roarke, and I never claimed to be military."

Those eyes burned instantly. Clearly, Raphael didn't enjoy lies or games. Or time wasted. He pushed away from the wall and came over to the exam table. He eyed the Healer. "All right, Billie?"

The woman with the dark, short hair and ivy-green eyes nodded.

"Almost done."

"They're fine," Killian told her, not liking the position he was in. On his back while the leader of the Pantera stood over him. "I'm an exceptional clotter."

"Oh, yeah," Billie answered with heavy sarcasm, holding him in place. "You're a real super soldier."

Her words caused his lip to curl. She had no fucking clue. "I'm not a solider."

"Maybe not anymore," Raphael said. "But you were."

Killian's gaze lifted and locked with the man.

"Everything about you says armed forces, Mr. O'Roarke. Build, attitude, fighting stance, and technique. And then there's the tattoo on your shoulder."

Killian's mouth thinned. "That has nothing to do with the military."

Pale brows lifted. "Doesn't it?"

What the hell? There was no possible way this man could know… Killian pulled his arm away just as the Healer finished her last stitch. "We're done. I need to speak to your leader alone."

"No we are not, you stubborn asshole," Billie countered, flashing him a green-eyed glare. "You need balm."

"I wouldn't argue with her," Raphael put in. "Or any Pantera female, actually. You'll just end up with—"

"Claw marks?" Killian supplied.

Raphael's lips twitched.

"If you're lucky." Billie snorted as she slapped some goo on his arm then quickly bandaged him. "You're welcome, by the way," she added as she got up and left the room.

"Your women are…interesting," Killian said as the door slammed shut.

"Females," Raphael corrected. "And yes, they are."

"Exceptionally strong. Bold. That…Rosalie." He sniffed, remembering how the wom—*female*—had both bloodied him and sat on top of him naked without even a hint of fear or embarrassment. "Definitely beautiful, but completely out of contr—"

"Don't speak of her." Raphael's eyes and his tone were grave now. "What she's been through, she's allowed to—"

Killian's brows knit together as the male cut himself off. "What has she been through?" *And why do I even give a shit? Maybe because you want some reason, other than that she hates humans, for how feral she was toward you.*

For a second, Raphael looked pissed at himself for saying anything. Then a forced mask of ease came over his expression. "It's really none of your concern, Mr. O'Roarke. Now. Tell me. What is it you want? And why didn't I let my Hunter gut you on the bank?"

"I think that's a question for both of us to answer, but I'll go first. I need your help."

"I don't offer help to humans who wander onto my land. Not anymore."

Killian expelled a heavy breath. He eyed the guards, who he knew weren't going anywhere, then turned back to Raphael. "If I was only human, I wouldn't have wandered onto your land."

Something that didn't seem like surprise flickered in Raphael's eyes. "What are you saying? You are human, Mr. O'Roarke. I smell you."

"But that's not all you smell, is it?"

"You are military," he said in a quiet voice.

"Was," Killian agreed.

Raphael's eyes closed for just a second. Pain registered on his face, in the set of his jaw and the furrow in his brow. When he finally opened them again, it wasn't pain Killian saw there, but Raphael's killer puma. "So they've done it," he ground out.

Killian's jaw tightened. The Pantera knew about the plans the secret black ops group operating within the military had to create an army of super soldiers. Well, of course they knew. Or at least their leader did.

"I was told it was therapy for some lingering PTSD I was going through," Killian explained through gritted teeth. "Injections. Isolation. Therapy. But every day I felt angrier, more combative. And at night, I dreamed…" He cursed under his breath.

"What?" Raphael pushed.

"That I was this massive black puma."

A muscle pulsed below the leader's right eye. "How many injections did they give you?"

"Twelve before I escaped and came here."

"And you came here because…" Raphael began with an edge to his tone. "What? You think you're one of us now? That you belong here?"

Anger pulled at Killian's insides. That same anger he'd felt in the lab. "I'm here, commander, because I *don't* want to be one of you."

Raphael stared at him.

"I'm here," Killian continued. "Because I need you to take whatever they put inside of me—out."

Raphael opened his mouth to speak, but before he did, the exam room door burst open. A man with a ton of tats and piercings, wearing a lab coat, strolled in. And following right behind him—*holy shit*—was none other than Kitten, aka Rosalie.

Aka, the one who'd nearly gutted his ass.

A flash of memory assaulted Killian's brain as he sat up in the bed. The ground near the bayou. Her on her back. Him on his back. Naked, sweaty, tantalizing flesh…

"Sorry, Raph," the tatted guy was saying. "I couldn't stop her."

"It's fine, Jean-Baptiste."

Jean-Baptiste raised his eyebrows, like *Are you sure? She's super pissed.* But after getting the nod from Raphael, he turned and headed back out.

"Rosalie?" Raphael began.

Killian turned to look at her, ran his gaze from the tips of her black combat boots, up her denim-clad legs to the short dark-gray sweater that exposed an inch of her trim belly. She was physical perfection. Drop dead. Dick to stone. Too bad she was hell-bent on killing him.

His gaze landed on her face. Skin like porcelain, hair the color of the morning sun, green eyes that tried to suck out your soul, and pink lips that were ready to swallow it right down.

"Unbelievable," she ground out, her eyes narrowed on the leader of her species.

"What is?" Raphael asked her calmly.

She jabbed a finger in Killian's direction. "You're keeping him, aren't you? *Sir.*"

The man's eyebrows lifted. "Keeping him? He's not a pet, Rosalie."

"Damn right, he's not," she returned. "He's the enemy. He fucking attacked me!"

"Okay, come on," Killian interrupted. "It was you who attacked me. Yanked my ass right out of the water. Got my back to the dirt, claws inside flesh. I'd think you'd be proud of the fact."

Her eyes cut to his, emerald fire bearing down on him. "Pride comes with a job well done, Human." One pale eyebrow jutted upward. "You're still breathing."

"Rosalie," Raphael warned.

"For now," she added.

Killian's mouth twitched with a grin. "Such hostility."

She sneered.

"He's not a pet," Raphael confirmed. "And he's not a prisoner.

But...he will remain under guard as we sort some things out."

"*Not* a prisoner?" she repeated, stunned.

"That's what I said."

Killian turned to the male. He wasn't telling Rosalie about the injections. About the reason Killian was here. Why? Were the other Pantera not aware of what was happening? About the super soldier program?

"Fine," she said tightly.

"Fine?" Killian repeated, his gaze finding hers once again. "The fight is over already?"

She ignored him and looked at Raphael. "I'll guard him."

Raphael practically snorted. "I don't think so."

Her lip curled. She had a very sexy mouth. "You need someone on him."

"I have two someones right here," Raphael said, pointing behind him to the male guards.

"They're Suits," she said, as if that explained everything. "You need a Hunter on this. Why not me?"

Raphael exhaled. "Honestly, I don't think you're stable enough."

Her expression went tight and she lifted her chin an inch. "What is that supposed to mean?"

"You'll kill him." The words were simple. Honest. Obvious. And Raphael didn't allow her to counter. "He has information we need. That I need."

She sniffed, disgusted. "Don't they all."

The leader of the Pantera didn't answer. His eyes were strangely kind as he stared at her. Killian wondered if the latitude he was giving her was due to that mysterious something that she'd been through.

Her shoulders drooped. "Don't you get it?" she continued, her tone softer now. "The humans, they don't give a shit about us, Raph. Or about sharing anything with us. They only want to destroy us. You keep letting them in here. Giving them chances. Working with them. When are you going to make them pay?"

"Your anger is understandable, Rosalie, but—"

"Don't give me any of that shit." She didn't say it with any amount of menace. But Raphael wasn't about to let her defiance slide this time.

"Watch yourself, Hunter." His eyes had darkened. "I believed that when you came to me about forgiving Hiss you'd let go of—"

"Hiss is Pantera," Rosalie cut in.

Killian sat up even taller. Who was this…Hiss?

"He showed me that when we broke into the lab." Her eyes swept over Killian. "I have no forgiveness for anything human."

Jaw tight, Raphael nodded. "Then go. And leave this one to me."

"No," Killian broke in.

They both turned to stare at him. "What?" Raphael asked.

"I want her." The words slid from his tongue like honey. Slow and easy. His eyes locked with Rosalie's. "If you insist on someone shadowing me, guarding me while I'm here, then I want her."

The leader cursed, low and black. "I can't allow it. She wants your blood."

Killian laughed. "I'm sure she's not the only one. At least she's honest about it. I know where she stands."

Green eyes flickered with heat, but if it was sexual interest or the possibility of getting him alone and removing his heart with her puma's teeth, he couldn't tell.

"It's settled, then," she said, her lips curving into a smile.

"Nothing is settled until I say it is," Raphael returned tightly. "Rosalie, if this man ends up dead, you will not be able to remain in the Wildlands. Do you understand me?"

She gasped and turned to look at the leader of her kind.

"Do you want to take that risk?" he asked.

Her jaw tightened, but she nodded.

"I need your word, Hunter," he pushed.

"He will not die, Raphael. I give you my word." *But he might feel some pain*, her eyes said.

Killian could handle pain. He might even enjoy it if it was coming from her.

"And," Raphael said just as she was turning Killian's way, "no puma."

She whirled back to face him, eyes wide, nostrils flared.

"When you're around him, the cat is caged."

Her face reddened. "Why?"

"You know why," he stated pointedly, piquing Killian's curiosity. What was this about? So much mystery surrounding the beautiful and terrifying Rosalie. "Now, take him over to the garden house."

"That's very near your home," she said, looking confused. "Why not one of the secure units?"

"Take him, Hunter."

She growled softly. "Fine. Follow me, Human."

With a nod at the leader of the Pantera, Killian grabbed his now-dry shirt and pushed off the bed. As Rosalie walked out the door, her strides confident, her ass swinging from side to side, a thought slammed into his mind before he could stop it. *Follow you? Anywhere, Kitten. Any-fucking-where.*

# Chapter 3

She'd been to the garden house only once. It was about an acre away from Raphael and his mate Ashe's two-story antebellum, and overrun with vines and flowers and late tomatoes climbing up the porch railings. The last resident had been an older female who'd kept mostly to herself and had loved everything green and growing, so the exterior of the small two-bedroom cottage appeared to be constructed almost entirely of moss and spotted bee balm. Under the cover of night, the scent of all the living things was intoxicating.

But Rosalie only scented human.

"Are you really going to stand outside the house all night?"

Her back to the front door, Rosalie stared straight ahead, across the long expanse of moonlit yard. The human male had been trying to engage her since they'd arrived an hour ago, this time coming to the open window to speak to her.

"You've gotta be hungry," he added.

She said nothing. Just as she'd said nothing when Raphael, Genevieve, and Lian had brought over food and supplies. While the leader of the Pantera spoke with Killian, the Suit female and the Hunter had tried like hell to not only discuss the human, but get her to relinquish her post as his guard. Lian had even offered to take her place. Said any of the Hunters would. But she'd refused them with a shake of the head.

They thought she'd break. Would give in to her puma's desire for human blood and get sent away from the Wildlands for it. She understood their worry, and she appreciated their care. But no one "handled" Rosalie except Rosalie.

"There's a great spread in here," the human called.

She rolled her eyes. Forget the human part—this man was going to *irritate* her into killing him. "No thanks," she ground out. "Unless you're offering me your blood."

"And if I am…?"

"Then you'll be dead before dessert."

"You know you just smiled when you said that, right?"

Her lips twitched. Again. "I don't doubt it."

He released a breath. "Come on. Eat with me."

"No."

"Rosalie—"

Her head came around fast and she hissed at him. "Don't call me that. You don't get to call me that."

He wasn't at all put out by her ferocity. "What should I call you, then?" His thick, dark eyebrows lifted. "Hunter? Mistress?" He grinned. "Kitten?"

Oh, the puma wanted out so badly... "Listen, Human. I'm not coming in there and eating with you. Period. End of discussion."

"All right." He shrugged, then left the window, disappeared inside the house.

Finally. She heaved a sigh of relief. She didn't like being around him. Not just because he was human, one of *them*. But because, unfortunately, she found him attractive. She shook her head. *Very attractive.* Like when he spoke, she watched the way his lips moved.

Goddess, she didn't deserve to breathe. For the fifth time since leaving Medical, she asked herself why she was doing this. Guarding the human. Why she'd insisted on it. Especially after Raphael had made her swear she wouldn't hurt him. Well, kill him is what she'd actually promised. But one would surely lead swiftly to the other, wouldn't it?

Why hadn't she walked away right when the leader had announced the human was staying? She should be patrolling the border, looking for more of them. Groups of them. Enemies of the Pantera.

The screen door pressed against her back then, and instantly she whirled around, her puma ready to spring. *Down girl. You're not getting me kicked out of my home. Not today.*

"Making a break for it, Human?" she snarled as the door opened and Killian emerged.

"For the porch, absolutely," he returned, moving past her with a snort.

She watched him as he headed for the faded floral loveseat with the small table in front of it and proceeded to set up dinner. A dinner for two. He was wearing the new clothes Lian had brought over: a pair of jeans and a blue Guns N' Roses T-shirt. Granted, this man was no Pantera male, but he surely equaled one in size. From his height, to the bulging biceps, to the way the shirt clung to hard abs and how tight his ass looked in that denim.

Her lip curled with disgust. But at the same time her belly warmed. *No. Just...no.* "You're not allowed to leave the residence, Human."

"I don't know how you divvy property here in your Wildlands, but where I come from this is still the residence."

"Where you come from." She sniffed. "They have porches attached to Locke's laboratories now, do they?"

"Who's Locke?"

She rolled her eyes. "Please."

He didn't say anything for a second. He was pouring lemonade into glasses. But when he took a seat, he said, "Iowa."

"What?"

He turned to look at her, those blue eyes annoyingly friendly. "I'm from Iowa. Originally. Farming family. Mostly soybeans."

She stared at him. She didn't want to know this. Any of this. Personal information. It made one weak and vulnerable to attack. She would never be weak again. Her stomach growled.

"Oh come on," he said. "Your body's in a state of revolt. This fried chicken's delicious. And it'll tide you over until something more human comes along."

She sneered at him. "The only human I'm interested in eating is you."

Rosalie didn't realize how that sounded until the man's mouth curved up into one of the sexiest smiles she'd ever seen. Then she wanted to just curl up in a ball and roll right off the porch.

But of course she didn't. She lifted her chin and said arrogantly, "You know what I mean."

His blue eyes flashed. "You're scared to get too close to me." He nodded. "Understandable."

"No. That's not it. At all."

"You sure?" He smiled, then started making soft clucking sounds.

She shook her head and heaved a sigh. "You're super annoying."

Didn't stop him from continuing on.

"Also, that's really inappropriate when you're actually eating the chicken."

His grin only widened as he clucked.

"Oh, fine!" she heaved, walking over and grabbing a chicken leg off the table. "I'll eat if you stop."

He did, then patted the seat beside him. "Come on, Hunter. I won't bite."

"Of course you won't," she said, tearing into the chicken as she remained standing. She was starving. Hadn't realized how starving until right that moment. "You're a weak-blooded human."

He tossed her the side-eye. "Who had you bound and on your back in under a minute."

She glared at him.

He grinned. Again. "Can I ask you something, Kitten?"

"'Hunter' is fine."

He pouted for one quick second, then said, "I understand the dislike of humans now that your world has been outed, and they're filled with curiosity and fear. I understand the distrust. But your hate runs deep. Blood deep. Why?"

Her insides clenched. "Hand me that lemonade."

He did, but didn't let up on the questions. "Raphael alluded to something...something you're going through."

Rosalie reached for a biscuit, though her stomach was in knots. "You're right. This food is good."

He sniffed. "Okay. Got it. None of my business."

Damn right it wasn't. But not only that, she refused to go personal with this human. It was the first rule of guarding a prisoner, which he pretty much was. You don't ask or answer anything that could make you vulnerable.

But as she finished off her biscuit, she broke that rule. "So, you grew up on a farm?"

"Yup," he said, taking a bite of an apple. "Loved it. Open air, miles and miles of land. It was simple."

"Sounds pretty perfect."

He nodded. "Was."

"So why did you leave?" *And head for Locke's lab? Glory? Money?*

"My parents passed away in an accident my senior year of high school. After I graduated, I just didn't want to stay, you know? They were the only family I had, and it was lonely..."

Her heart squeezed a bit. Loss was really something they shared. "I'm sorry."

He nodded. "I sold the place to a nice family. Then, I joined the army."

Rosalie's head came around so fast she nearly gave herself whiplash. All softness and understanding gone, she stared at him. His jaw was tight, like he knew what he'd just said would be controversial.

Controversial? Try outrageous!

"You're a solider?" she ground out, her appetite now gone. There it was. She'd only been guessing that he might be from one of Locke's labs, but this… "Does Raphael know?"

"Yes."

Shit. That's why the leader had wanted this man to stay. Needed all the information. "Why did you come here? What do you want from Raphael? From us?"

He turned to look at her. His eyes were shuttered now. Back to the shark who was giving nothing away. "That's between Raphael and myself. For now. If he wants someone to know, he'll tell them."

*Someone*? "I'm not just someone." She stood up. "You're part of them," she snarled. "Those bastards. Fuck you!" Goddess, her cat was pushing to get out. And she wanted to let it. Let the puma handle this. Let the puma handle everything. "We're not helping you people create some hybrid monster for your battlefields."

His eyes flashed with anger and his lips parted to retort. But before a word was uttered, he took stock in her demeanor. Her barely controlled demeanor. He was off the loveseat and at her side in an instant. "Are you all right?"

Fuck, she was shaking. Like a scared cub. Couldn't stop herself. But she refused his touch. "Get away from me."

"You look like you're going to pass out."

"No, *Human*," she snarled at him. "I look like my puma is trying to get out and tear you to shreds."

She expected him to step away. Hell, he should be running into the house and locking the door, if he was smart. But instead he courted death and did the most insane thing ever. He pulled her into his arms.

Rosalie stiffened, growled, "What the hell are you doing?"

"Isn't it obvious?" he asked, pulling her even closer.

"Only if you have that rope again." Something strange was happening. Her puma was suddenly nowhere to be found, and the female part of her was…breathless…

He laughed softly, his hand moving in slow circles on her back. "I'm not trying to contain you, Hunter. Just give you a bit of comfort."

"I don't need comfort," she uttered, her tone strangled.

"I think you do."

She cursed through her uneven breathing. "You are so…human."

"Damn right I am." He made a low sound in his throat, and the rumble went from his chest into hers. It was… Goddess, it was—

*No!* No, this was wrong. Why wasn't she pulling away? Biting his shoulder? Taking off his ear? Desperate for blood? Why were her nostrils flaring? And why were her lungs pulling in his scent as though they couldn't bear to have anything else inside them?

The human was the first to pull back, release her. But he didn't look happy about it. In fact, he looked confused and troubled. *Join the club.*

His expression tight, he stared down at her. "Is the cat okay?"

*Okay?* Goddess, nothing was okay. About this. About him. About her. And where was her cat? Her protection? The one thing that was always there to stomp out feelings and emotions and...attraction?

Rosalie gazed up into those deep blue eyes. Okay? The cat was more than okay. It was...quiet.

With a surge of deep fear and guilt, she pulled completely away from him and stalked over to the door. Held it open. "Time for bed, Human."

One dark brow lifted over those ever-changing eyes, but he didn't say anything. Instead, after a few seconds, he went and gathered up all the food, then walked past her into the house.

"'Night, Hunter," he said in a pensive tone that mirrored the feelings running through her.

After the door closed, she pressed back against it and tried to breathe normally again. But it was no use. Her throat felt tight now, scratchy. Her lungs didn't seem to be making enough air. What was wrong with her? Why had she allowed herself to be touched...hugged? And why did she want to call that human back again right this very minute and tell him to call her...Rosalie?

# Chapter 4

*"Stay away!" Tim Donohue shouted, barely visible in the rubble. "Fuck, O'Roarke!"*

*Exhausted, eyes burning, Killian dragged an unconscious Mac Fields another three feet out of the wrecked building, then left him with the others. One more. Just one more.*

*"Stop!" Tim screamed at him. "Another one's coming, man!"*

*Killian didn't listen. You don't leave a comrade. Never leave a comrade. Not even with the threat of an IED.*

*Something nicked his arm. Fuck! The sting. He'd been hit. Suddenly, rounds of gunfire broke out less than forty meters away. No cover. Shit!*

*His men. He had to get to his men.*

*He had to hunt. Hunt the enemy!*

*But Tim...*

*An incoming round zoomed past his head. Eyes right and left. Nowhere to take cover. No-fucking-where!*

*"You gotta do this for me, man," Tim yelled. "Tell my wife I love—"*

*The blast of the IED sent Killian flying back. He hit the ground hard, air stolen from his lungs, blood leaking from his arm. When he looked up, Tim's head was down.*

*And he was silent.*

A gasp woke Killian. Not his own. Or was it? Eyes open, he realized where he was and who he was on top of. Shaking, sweat coating his skin, he rolled off her instantly. "Shit, I'm sorry."

He lay there on his back, breathing hard, staring at the ceiling, remembering where the fuck he was, totally exposed to whatever Rosalie wanted to do to punish him for assaulting—

He blinked, shook the sleep—the nightmares—from his mind for a second, then... He turned his head to look at her. "Why are you in my room?"

He'd taken the smallest one, stripped down to his underwear and fallen asleep around midnight. Alone.

She was sitting up. Wearing sweats and a tight tank top, her blonde hair loose around her shoulders. If he wasn't kind of pissed off at her in that moment—and shit, coming down from another memory mind-fuck—he might consider running his fingers through that hair.

"You were yelling," she said. "In your sleep. You sounded like someone was ripping your heart out. I was trying to wake you up."

*Oh, fuck.* She'd heard him...

He scrubbed a hand over his face. "I'm surprised you came in." He sort of half laughed, though in that moment it didn't seem all that funny. "Isn't ripping out my heart the very thing you're trying to do?"

"No."

"Only because you made a promise to your senior officer."

"He's not my senior officer."

"Right. Your leader. *El Presidenté.*"

She didn't say anything to that. In fact, she was way quieter than normal. Maybe he'd done more than yell. Maybe he'd said something...about combat or a mission. Or shit, his time in the lab. Well, he wasn't getting into any of that. Not until he knew what Raphael was going to do, or offer him.

"Well, as you can see, I'm fine," he said. "All intact."

Her eyes ran over him. To check. Or maybe for another reason. Whatever it was, it made his gut clench, and shit below his waist fill with enough blood to be obvious.

"You can go," he continued, not liking the idea of pitching a tent in front of her. "Back to your guard station."

But she didn't move. She sat there on the bed, looking all hot and sexy with her tight tank top, no bra, hair all wild and eyes that kept darting his way.

Yep, full hard-on now.

"Rosalie," he began. "Sorry, Hunter—"

"I have nightmares, too."

Killian stilled, not sure he'd heard her correctly. "What's that?"

"Or I did have them..." she continued. She sighed. "They were a lot like that. Like yours. No words, just..." Her eyes lifted to meet his. "Pain."

He stared at her, couldn't believe she was sharing anything with him. Much less something so personal.

"I don't know what you're doing here, Human—" she started.

"Killian."

"Human," she returned. "But I know real pain when I hear it."

Shit. What was this? He really wanted to know. Wanted to ask. But he didn't. He was pretty sure she wouldn't tell him anyway. "So they're gone?" he asked. "The nightmares?"

She nodded. "When I let my cat form take over. Sleep in it twenty-four/seven."

But Raphael hadn't wanted her in the cat form. Said she would kill him if she was. So… Killian sat up on one elbow. "But you can't be in your cat form when you're around me."

Her eyes met his. "Really?"

"Why don't you stop this, Hunter? Let someone else guard me. Go back to what you were doing. Go back to your puma and…sleep." His eyes roamed over her beautiful but very guarded face. "That really made the dreams stop?"

She nodded.

With a sniff of derision, Killian mumbled under his breath, "Maybe I should give it a try."

But she heard him. "Humans can only be human, Human."

"Yeah, you'd think, wouldn't you?" he ground out.

Her eyes narrowed. "Tell me why you're here."

"Help," he said.

"What kind? Immunity? Did you do something on the outside? Are you trying not to go back into combat? Do you know something about the military's plans for the Pantera and our very unique and highly sought-after DNA?"

He remained silent.

Which pissed her off. Not like that was a hard thing. "You're a soldier," she snarled. "But you don't know who Locke is. You're a human, but you're not a criminal or Raphael wouldn't have let you—" She stopped, blinked at him. Killian could see her mind working, and it was fast and sharp. "When I came up on you and the rat in the bayou…I didn't scent human right away. Only Pantera."

"Is that right?" he said softly.

Her lips parted then, and she leaned in. All the way until the tip of her nose brushed his throat. Killian inhaled sharply. He didn't know what she was pulling off him, but her scent was intoxicating. Like a rare flower, whose fragrance existed only for him. He growled at the ridiculous, romanticized, almost insane thought. But when her nose moved up to his jaw and her breath caressed his neck, he lost all brain function whatsoever. His hunger, his desire were on a level he'd never experienced before. An almost animalistic...

*Fuck. No.*

Slowly, she started to sniff him. His jaw, his ear, the corner of his mouth.

"What do you scent, Hunter?" he uttered in a voice he didn't recognize.

She drew back a few inches, her eyes finding his. They were confused and anxious, and...hot. She bit her lower lip, giving his already hard cock another surge of blood, and whispered, "Pantera."

Before he knew what he was doing, Killian's hand stole around her head, fisting into her hair as he pulled her in for a kiss. The instant their mouths connected, he groaned. It was like having every fucking fantasy he'd ever had since puberty come to life. She was so warm, hungry, and proved the latter with her tongue when he turned his head and deepened their kiss. Christ, he'd never experienced anything so stunning. Like fireworks going off inside him. Constantly. Each one more perfect than the last.

Each one driving him insane with lust.

He fell back onto the pillow, taking her with him. And she responded instantly. Getting on top of him, straddling him, growling at him as he worked her mouth. He left her hair and plunged both hands underneath her tank top. Hot, smooth skin assaulted his unworthy hands. She groaned into his mouth and arched into his touch. The need to flip her onto her back, strip her naked, and drive his cock deep inside her was so intense, he had to fight with himself about it.

And shit, if he was going to admit it, fight with something else too...

He raked his palms up both sides of her waist, up her ribcage, until he felt the soft curve of her breasts. His chest ached to feel her pressed against him. And his cock, fuck, his cock was already leaking at the tip. Anticipation. His own personal hell. He cursed his need into her mouth as she lifted her chest just enough for him to slip his hands underneath and capture her breasts.

Shit, he was going to lose it.

And why did that "thing" inside him keep snarling the word *mine* over and over again? Maybe because it wanted her. All of her. Every inch. First with his hands, then his tongue—then his cock.

He kneaded her breasts, played with them as he played with her tongue and sucked it into his mouth. Rosalie held back nothing, and he loved it. She had his thigh between her legs and was dry-fucking him.

No. Not dry at all. Very, very wet, even with the cotton sweats between them.

As one hand teased her nipple, Killian slipped the other under the waistband of her sweats. It wasn't easy. She was grinding against him. So strong. Christ, he was into her strength. It was so goddamned hot.

*She* was so goddamned hot.

The second his hand met smooth, wet pussy, Killian was gone. On another planet. One he wanted to exist on for eternity. He slid his finger through her warm lips and found her clit swollen and ready. As he consumed her mouth, played her nipple and stroked her clit, he listened to the sounds she made against his lips. Moans of pleasure, snarls of animalistic hunger.

And he understood the language of both.

Leaving his thumb to work the needy bud, Killian slipped two fingers inside her pussy. Instantly her hot, tight walls clamped around him, suckling him. Jesus…he was going to fucking come without her having even touched him.

"I feel it," he uttered against her mouth as he started to thrust inside her. "Come for me, Rosalie."

She froze.

Utterly and completely.

From the top of her head to her feet.

And so did Killian.

"What…" he uttered. "What's wrong?"

She was scrambling off him before the last word was even out of his mouth.

"What the hell?" he said, sitting up. Shit, she was off the bed, her back to him. "Are you okay?"

She didn't have to say the word *no*. He could feel that word radiating off her shaking body. What had he done?

"Never. Never again." She glanced over her shoulder and gave him a look of such hate, he felt it in his marrow. "Human."

She slammed the door when she walked out.

Leaving Killian to stare after her.

His second nightmare of the night.

# Chapter 5

As the sun awoke in the sky before her, guilt and self-hatred swam in Rosalie's blood. Not only had she let another male kiss and touch her, but he was a human. She refused to believe what she'd scented last night. He may have been infused with something to try and pass as a Pantera, but he was no true puma shifter. He was human. The very species that had taken her mate from her. Tears threatened, but she pushed them back. She didn't deserve the sweet relief they would bring. She deserved the cold morning air assaulting her still-heated skin. She deserved exhaustion. She deserved the hard wood surface of the porch steps against her ass.

She deserved pain.

"Have you been sitting out here all night?"

She glanced up. Backlit by the early morning's light, Raphael was coming up the walkway. He looked totally put-together in a dark-gray suit, crisp white shirt, and maroon tie. All business. As usual.

"Just doing my job, sir," she said with a mock salute.

"And yet you didn't scent me until I was almost on top of you," he said, stopping at the bottom step.

She laughed. Bitterly. "You and Ashe have a nice romantic morning?" When his eyes widened slightly, she nodded. "Oh, I scented you, sir. From the second you walked out your front door."

His gaze moved over her, assessing as he always did. "Are you all right, Rosalie?"

"Never better," she answered with a false smile. "So, are you here for the prisoner? Am I taking him to the border and kicking his ass out of the Wildlands?"

"No."

"Didn't think so." She shook her head, slowly. "Am I taking him to his lovely new cabin near the bayou, serving him breakfast, and welcoming him to the Wildlands as an honored guest?"

The male pushed out a breath. "What you're going to do is go home."

She grunted.

"Get some sleep," he continued. "Take a shower and report to Parish at midday."

"Fuck that," she tossed out.

"Rosalie," he said, his nostrils flaring as his chin lifted, "you're pushing me. Forcing me into disciplining you."

She snorted. "Boy, the daddy thing is really going to your head. How is little Soyala, by the way?" One brow lifted sardonically. "I imagine an excellent sleeper, by the way you smell."

"Your anger is growing out of control."

"You have no idea." The words rushed from her mouth without thought. Instantly, she wished she could bite them back because Raphael's expression changed from aggravated to worried in an instant.

"You need to see one of the Healers," he said,

*Yep. Biting them back would've been awesome.* "I'm curious, Raphael," she said calmly. "Would you say that to me if I was a male?" She stood up. "Or would you pat me on the back, invite me out for a drink at The Cougar's Den, then halfway through a game of pool tell me I should get laid?"

Most males would've gotten immediately defensive, but Raphael was totally unaffected by her candor—or her baiting, depending on how one looked at it. "I treat grief as it should be treated, Hunter. With compassion, care, understanding, *and* a kick in the ass if needed. Male or female. Now." He gave her a pointed look. "Go home."

"The human is mine to guard," she fought. "Until he no longer needs it."

"Why?"

"What do you mean *why*? It's my job. I'm doing my job." She sounded as though she barely believed it herself.

"And I'm doing mine," Raphael said softly. "Go home. Lian will take over."

"No," came a male voice behind them. "Rosalie stays with me."

Both Rosalie and Raphael turned to find Killian standing at the doorway. Shit, she hadn't scented him, but she sure *saw* him. Hungrily, her gaze ran over his six-foot-something frame. Jeans, black tank, hard muscle, bare feet, wet hair. A rush of lust shot through her body as her mind conjured images of herself on her knees, pulling down that zipper with her teeth.

Sudden, unwanted tears pricked at her eyes with the thought, and she quickly swiped at them with her hand. She was in trouble. And the kind she'd never had to deal with before. She needed to stop fighting. Follow Raphael's orders and go home. Shower. Sleep. Get her head on straight and never see this human again. He was screwing with her mind. Had since he'd crawled up onto the shore like a gorgeous laboratory-grown mistake.

Goddess, she needed her cat. Her heart jumped inside her chest. If she walked away from this, from him, she could walk away in her puma form. As long as she wasn't around the human—

"You seem to think you have a say in this, Mr. O'Roarke," Raphael returned, his tone cool.

"Maybe I do," he said casually, but Rosalie didn't miss the dogged set of his shoulders and jaw. "I'm about to let you dissect me, mentally and physically, and I only want two things out of it. The first you know. The second." His gaze flickered to Rosalie. "Unless she wants out, of course."

Rosalie felt the weight of both their stares and wanted to disappear. Behind Raphael's intense gaze was a need to understand, and concern. Lots of concern. And behind the human's… Attraction, challenge, curiosity.

What would she do? After last night's idiocy, what *should* she do? And Goddess, what had the human asked Raphael for?

So many questions. Ones she'd have to wait to have answered. Well, she had time.

"Where do you want him?" she asked the leader of the Pantera in that all-business tone he appreciated. "And when?"

As the seconds ticked by, it seemed as though the Head Suit might continue to argue the point with her. But, for whatever reason, he held off. "Have him at the clinic in thirty minutes. Jean-Baptiste and I will meet you there."

"Yes, sir."

She watched him go, stride across the lawn in his oh-so-fine suit, then she headed back into the house. Killian's scent was everywhere. In the air, the furniture…maybe even her lungs. She growled with irritation at the fact, yet followed it like a hungry cub into the kitchen. The man was seated at the table, tucked into a bowl of cereal. She went and stood over him, fuming.

"Problem, Hunter?" he asked, pouring milk onto his Lucky Charms. *Typical Lian, bringing that over here.* The Hunter was obsessed with that shit.

"I don't need you coming to my rescue," she ground out. "Human."

He glanced up. His jaw was brushed with dark morning beard. "Is that what you thought I was doing?"

Rosalie wondered what the stubble would feel like against her tongue. Around his mouth. Biting his bottom lip. He liked that...responded to—

*Fuck. Me.* "Just hurry up and finish," she growled.

He shook his head and went back to his cereal. "So I'm gathering we're not going to talk about last night."

She leaned against the wall and crossed her arms over her chest. "You mean the nightmare?"

"Honey, I'd never call you, your kisses, or what you did to me a nightmare." His eyes flashed with humor, and something else...

That something else made her nipples tighten.

"Eat," she hissed.

He took an enormous bite, crunching away, then asked, "Are you starving yourself again?"

"No. I already had breakfast."

"When?"

"Before the sun came up."

"Couldn't sleep, huh?" He nodded. "Yeah. I had a real *hard* time of it myself." He grinned before scooping up another spoonful of cereal.

She wanted to slap that grin right off his face!

No...wait. That's not what she wanted to do at all.

She wanted *to kiss* that grin right off his face. Then make him groan. Then let him make her groan...

Panic spread through her blood and she uttered a terse, "Be outside in five minutes."

She stormed from the room and out the front door, stopping only when she hit the top of the steps. She gripped the railing. Her heart was slamming against her ribs, her mouth was dry, and she wanted to cry. Again. Fucking pussy.

*Mercier...* She glanced up into the powder blue sky. *I'm sorry. I've betrayed you.*

# Chapter 6

"You're going to leave me with a few pints, right?" Killian asked the technician who'd just taken his tenth blood sample of the day.

Ford—the male with black eyes and a scar down the right side of his face—replied dryly, "Try and think of it like we're already removing our DNA from you."

Killian sniffed. "Just feels like you're bleeding me dry. Not exactly what I thought was going to happen."

Jean-Baptiste, who left the three other techs on the opposite side of the room to their computer screens and DNA processing and analysis equipment, walked over to him. "What were you thinking?"

"Well, I was hoping you'd have...an antidote. Something that could go right into my bloodstream and kill whatever they injected me with."

The massive, tatted-up doctor laughed. "Oh, if only it was that simple. We've got urine, saliva tests, MRI...but we're going to need more blood. Blood tells us everything. A basic metabolic panel to reveal any diseases you might have, how the organs are functioning. And then an analysis of proteins, DNA and RNA—see what's happening from those all-powerful injections."

"Sounds like you have some experience with this already," Killian said. "A protocol in place." Back in the lab, toward the latter part of his "stay," he'd heard talk of Pantera prisoners who had been experimented on. It was those days especially when he couldn't help despising his own species. Nothing was sacred. Not even life.

Raphael walked in then, took a quick look around, and headed straight for Killian.

"Do what you gotta do, Doc," Killian told Jean-Baptiste, dropping back against the pillow. "I think I'm going to be hanging out here a while."

"Five hours and counting." Raphael handed him a donut wrapped in a napkin. Chocolate glazed. Then pulled up a chair. "Eat it. It'll help."

"I'm fine, man."

"That's right. I forgot. Super solider." His brows lifted. "But loss of blood is loss of blood. No matter who or what we are."

*True that.* And his stomach was making all kinds of noise, so…he took a bite. Then another. "Thanks."

Raphael nodded. "Now, Benson Enterprises. What do you know about them?"

The male wasted no time. Not that Killian blamed him. They both wanted answers. "Benson was the name of the clinic. Given to me by my commanding officer when I requested an eval, or something to help with my PTSD."

The leader's pupils dilated. "Commanding officer's name?"

Killian stalled out for a second. The guy had a family, wife, and kids. He didn't want to—

"Just need all the information, Mr. O'Roarke," Raphael said as if reading his mind. "I've got to connect the dots."

Killian eyed the male. "I've known the guy for years, served under him. I'm sure he knew nothing about what was going to happen to me. He'd never send a man under his command into danger unprotected like that. I don't want him or his family hurt."

Raphael nodded.

Killian wasn't at all sure that the Pantera followed the same honor code he did, but they were trusting him, letting him inside their world. Helping him. Maybe he needed to do the same.

Killian released a breath, along with the name of his commander. "Brad Vanco."

The name didn't seem to register with the male, but he typed it into his phone anyway. "Had you heard of Benson Enterprises before Mr. Vanco mentioned it?"

"No."

"And when you went there, initially, who did you speak with?"

"The main doc was a woman. Marcia Copper. A head-shrinker. She was the one who insisted I stay at the facility. I just wanted to talk to someone. Therapy, maybe some meds to keep the nightmares at bay. But she insisted that this was the best way of doing things. Inpatient treatment." Killian's desire for the donut faded and he set it on the side table. "Then there was no choice on my part. It was like being a goddamned prisoner of war."

Raphael glanced up. "The coordinates you gave us for the lab—"

"Did you burn that piece of shit to the ground?" Killian interrupted with undisguised menace.

Raphael shook his head. "It was only an abandoned building."

Shock rolled through Killian and he sat up. "That's impossible. I was just there. Broke out two days ago."

"So you said. Are you sure that's where you were being held?"

"That's where I went when I came in for treatment."

Raphael paused for a second, his brow furrowed. "Was it possible you were moved? Without knowing it?"

His chest tightened as his mind was inundated with questions. "I would've known," he said to himself as well as to the leader of the Pantera. "I would've had to have known. Despite the labs and the room where I was held, The Christopher had this smell—"

"The Christopher," Raphael interrupted sharply. "What's that?"

"Sounds like a swank hotel, right? Like in Vegas or something. Shit, it was anything but." He shook his head. "Wasn't my thing. The guards, the techs, the docs, everybody called it that. Named after the guy who funded the place."

A cold, hard look stole over Raphael's face. "Did you ever meet this man?"

"I saw him around the lab. Granted, he was always with a military escort, so I never got close to him. I noticed him checking in with the doctors though, pushing the technicians for more data—"

"We've got to get that motherfucker," Raphael said on a snarl.

"That's who you're…" Killian trailed off.

A scent he recognized was drifting into his nostrils, and for a moment he was completely captivated by it. His eyes closed and his mouth opened, and inside his chest that…*thing*…rumbled to life. In the back of his mind, he heard Raphael speaking, but it was too far away. He wanted more of that scent. What was it? He grinned. Whatever it was, it belonged to him.

Suddenly, a hand clamped around his arm, causing his eyes to burst open. But instead of looking for the one who'd touched him, his gaze was completely pinned to the open doorway.

*Puma.*

*My puma.*

"Shit! Baptiste, what the hell did you do?"

"Nothing."

"He's shifting! How the…fuck!"

The voices were there. In the background. They didn't matter to him. Nothing mattered but the golden female, her green eyes calling to him. A growl escaped his throat.

"It's her," Jean-Baptiste exclaimed. "Rosalie. She's in the hall. In her puma state."

The last thing Killian remembered before his mind dissolved was the deep hunger of the animal inside him.

Wanting out.

Wanting her.

# Chapter 7

Fur as black as the night.

Eyes so pale blue they reminded her of ice.

Rosalie watched as Killian's puma paced inside the cage.

*Puma.*

How was this possible? He was human. So human. And yet, she'd scented him last night, and at the bayou. Goddess, maybe she'd believed he'd been *played* with, like the rats. But she hadn't believed him capable of this. Shifting into a full-blooded puma. It wasn't possible. Except maybe it was. Raphael would tell her what he knew, explain things to her.

Right before he grounded her ass, or kicked it out of the Wildlands, that is.

She curled her hands around the bars of the large cage and stared at the gorgeous puma, who she was pretty sure didn't understand what was happening. Poor guy. Learning to separate the puma from the Pantera mind took practice. From the time you were a cub, you tried to break that code. And right now, Killian was pushed to the back, and all that occupied the cage was animal.

Her shoulders fell as she scented Raphael. *Shit hitting fan, here we come.* Goddess, she was such a moron.

He came to stand beside her. Didn't look at her. Instead, he stared at the pacing cat. "What were you thinking?" he asked in a dangerously quiet voice.

*That I'm a moron?* "That I could have a little time in my cat," she said aloud. "The human was with you and Baptiste and the other Healers. Surrounded. And for hours." She broke off, shaking her head—confident in what was coming next.

"Fine. Understandable and acceptable." He turned to face her. "*Outside* the clinic."

*Moron!*

"Why did you come back here, Rosalie?" he pressed. "To him, in your puma state?"

She looked over at the leader of the Suits, knowing her eyes were a perfect mirror into her confused soul. "I don't know." She shook her head. "I wanted to check on him?"

"Is that a question?"

"No," she said on a sigh.

"You care about him."

She shook her head. "No."

"You're attracted to him."

"Please stop." Her cheeks were burning. Thankfully, Killian couldn't hear this. Or could he? She didn't want to look to closely at him to find out.

"Your job was to keep him safe, Rosalie."

Her heart squeezed painfully, but she nodded. She'd screwed up big time. Granted, Killian wasn't dead, but this was huge nonetheless. She prayed Raphael would only suspend her from hunting duties or shit, toss her in one of the secure units. Because leaving the Wildlands... Goddess, her home—that would be unbelievably painful. And yet, she'd set herself up for punishment. What was wrong with her? Making foolish mistakes. Living inside her puma. Scared, angry—filled with grief and guilt all the time. It was no damn life that she was living. But she'd made her bed, so to speak. If Raphael went hardcore on her, well, she wouldn't walk out of the Wildlands crying for herself or begging for a second chance. She was a proud Pantera, after all.

She turned to go. "I'll prepare to leave."

Raphael grabbed her arm and cursed to himself. "No."

Her heart stuttered as she turned back to face him.

He shook his head. "For now, you're on probation. Until I decide what I'm going to do." He glanced back at the cat that was Killian and released a weighty breath. "You may hate humans for all the right reasons, Rosalie, but this one wasn't a part of what happened to Mercier."

She felt the tears again. Behind her eyes. In her throat. But she refused them. "How can you be sure of that?"

"I had him checked out. Had his story checked out. He's a good man. Fought for his country, saved many of his fellow soldiers, and went into a program he believed would help him deal with his grief over losing a close friend."

She remembered the dream—the nightmare he'd had. He couldn't get back to his...friend. "But the program didn't help him, did it?"

Raphael shook his head. "Was a false front. A way to experiment on soldiers without their knowledge or consent."

A lump formed in her throat, and for the first time in a long time, she didn't wish for her cat. They'd used him. Just like they'd used her and Mercier, and so many others. It was time to face and accept the truth... Humans weren't the enemy. It was Christopher and Benson Enterprises, and all those who turned a blind eye to the lives they were destroying.

She lifted her gaze to meet Raphael's. "I think I need some help. To deal with my grief. While I await my fate." Tears broke and swam in her eyes. But this time she didn't try to hide them or wipe them away.

A soft smile touched the Pantera leader's mouth and he covered her hand with his own. "You deserve to be happy, Rosalie. Mercier would've wanted nothing less."

Just hearing his name...she was about to break. "I'm going to go. Check in with Parish. All the Hunters. I have some...apologies to make."

He nodded. "I'll let you know when I've come to a decision."

She turned around to leave, but before she even got halfway to the door, the snarl of Killian's puma stopped her in her tracks. She didn't have to turn around to know what was happening, what he was feeling. Want he wanted.

Her.

In the room.

Close by.

And when he started to rage, go insane inside his cage, she could do nothing but oblige him.

# Chapter 8

When Killian came to, or awoke, or whatever it was that was happening to him, he felt like he'd been hit by a truck. His eyes were heavy and his mouth felt dry. He glanced around. He was in the same room, lying on the same gurney-style bed. Same…people. But there were no IV's or needles or tubes in his arms, and it felt…late. Felt like…night, if you could actually feel that without having visual access to the outside world.

He spotted the technician with the scar, reading a chart and typing something into a computer.

"You took too damn much," Killian said, though his voice was pretty much a whisper. And his throat hurt. What the hell?

"What's that?" Ford asked, glancing up.

"Blood," Killian ground out. "You took too much. Passed out."

The guy's brows lifted, but his eyes descended—back to the file and the computer.

"And with all the donuts I gave you." It was Raphael's voice. He was walking over to Killian's bedside, his mouth curved up in a sardonic smile. "Pussy."

That elicited a soft yet painful chuckle from Killian. "There was one donut. And, if I remember correctly, I only ate half of it." He gave the leader of the Pantera a strange, I'm-fucking-confused look. "My throat's killing me, man. In fact," he winced, "my whole body feels like it's been run over by a Humvee. Did I fall off the bed or get into a fight or something?"

"No." The male's expression tightened.

Okay, something was going on here. Something was wrong. Maybe it had to do with the tests on his blood. Maybe they'd found a way to take the DNA from him. Shit, maybe that's what the pain was from...they'd already done it. But then why—

His mind came to an abrupt halt. Not only was the most delectable scent in the world wafting into his nostrils, but every cell in his body was screaming that it belonged to him. Fucking strange. Then Rosalie walked into the room and strange upgraded to downright bizarre.

He let his gaze move over her. She was wearing jeans and a tight black tank top. Her hair was piled on top of her head, and her eyes—those sexy, green daggers—met his right away. His gut clenched. The same expression he'd seen in Raphael's gaze a second ago was shimmering in the Hunter's. Something like "*Shit's gone down and we're not sure how to tell you.*"

"Okay," he started, sitting up in the bed, shaking off the lightheaded thing that was making him feel like a weak-ass recruit on the first day of boot camp. "What the hell is going on here? Am I cured? Am I dying? Did the gallons of blood you took from me give you any clue—"

"Killian."

He shivered and groaned. It was Rosalie saying his name.

*Rosalie.*

And her face was all...what was that? Sympathy?

Shit. Maybe he really was dying.

He glanced over at Raphael, who was stone-faced and silent, then his eyes came back to Rosalie. "Why are you calling me that?" he demanded on a low growl.

She bit her lip. The lower one. Something he'd love to do. But not now. Not here. Maybe when the pain in his body eased up a bit he'd see if she was agreeable. *Screw that. She's worth the pain.*

"It's your name," she said.

"Not to you," he countered. "I'm Human, remember?"

Her gaze flickered to Raphael as she headed over to the chair beside Killian's bed and sat down. What the hell was going on? It was like a damn funeral in progress.

"Somebody better tell me something," he began with a slight snarl. "Or shit's going to get—"

Rosalie jumped in. "When you were...out—"

"Passed out?" he corrected.

"Yes."

"What? I snored? You watched? Or, maybe you took advantage of me?" he said with a dark edge.

"No." Her cheeks flushed as her eyes dipped to take in his naked chest and low-hanging gray sweatpants.

*Damn.* Those sweatpants were about to get tight if she kept that up. He cocked his head to the side and whispered, "You *wanted* to take advantage of me?"

"No."

"Your mouth says no, Hunter, but your eyes say—"

"You shifted into a puma!" she blurted out.

The room went still and Killian's heart ceased beating. Or it sure as shit felt that way. As he tried to remember how lungs worked, how breathing worked, he replayed the words she'd just tossed at him. Then again. There were only five of them, but that packed a significant punch. He felt strangely empty inside. Hollow. His mind too. Except for the five words. He started to shake his head. This could not be true. She was lying to him. Or he was still knocked out and this was a nightmare.

Another fucking nightmare.

His eyes captured hers and compelled her to speak or explain or... But—nothing. She wouldn't give him a damn thing. Raphael either. The room just remained silent.

For another five seconds, anyway. Then—

"What the fuck did you guys do to me?" Killian exploded, leaping off the bed. "You were supposed to take it out! Not turn it on! Fuck!" Thank Christ he wasn't wearing one of those hospital gowns. He would've ripped the shit off and been standing there buck naked.

Raphael and Ford looked appropriately sympathetic but crouched slightly—ready for whatever was coming their way. And that thing inside Killian? That hybrid monster that Rosalie had talked about? Yeah, that thing in his gut or chest? It moved, woke.

The puma.

A sneer touched his upper lip. Was that really his truth now? His state of being? How could he accept that?

"It wasn't them," Rosalie said, her voice even and strong.

Eyes pinned to the two males, Killian shook his head. "Bullshit."

"It wasn't, Killian," she continued. "It was...me."

Killian's head came around fast. She was standing up now, across the bed from him. Breathing hard, his heart slamming against his ribs, he glared at her.

"I came by your room, in my puma form," she explained.

"It…triggered something in you." She shook her head. "I don't understand why it would. I mean, there are plenty of puma females—"

"You don't understand?" Killian exclaimed. "Why you would trigger something in me?" He shook his head, snarled at her. "After last fucking night?"

She immediately blanched. "Don't—"

"I'm attracted to you, Hunter!" he continued. "Goddammit! You walked out on me last night, and today you come back in your puma form? You really do want to kill me, don't you?"

"This is inside you, Mr. O'Roarke," Raphael said before Rosalie could answer, his tone calm, sensible, though his body language warned there'd be a battle if Killian got any more out of control than he already was. "Benson Enterprises put it there, and I'm afraid we can't remove it."

"Now," Killian ground out, feeling out of his mind, out of control. "Right? You can't remove it now that I've shifted into one of you. There's no way to reverse course."

"The shift isn't the reason for the permanent state," Ford put in. "I believe, as does Jean-Baptiste, that this started to take form with the first injection." His eyes were firm, but kind. "I'm sorry, Mr. O'Roarke."

The dark, desperate emotions inside Killian rolled and pitched like a boat on an angry sea. He wanted to attack the technician, even Raphael. He wanted to spill blood and tear apart the room. And then he wanted to turn on the Hunter.

His eyes caught and held hers. Whatever she saw in his blue orbs made her cheeks flame and her nostrils flare. Not fear, not desire—but something definitely and ferociously in between.

He took a step toward her…

"It's late," Raphael intervened quickly. "You should have something to eat, Killian. Get some sleep. We'll talk more in the morning. Discuss your options."

"My options," Killian uttered blackly, his eyes still pinned to the Hunter.

"There are some, I assure you. Come on, Rosalie. Let's leave the male to process."

She swallowed thickly but did as her leader instructed, yanking her gaze from Killian's and walking past him and out the door.

He called me *the male*, Killian thought blackly, as he stared after her. *Like I'm one of them.* No longer a man. No longer a human. No longer recognizable.

His gaze found Ford's and he growled at him. Like the *male* he was. Like the animal he was. What this really happening? What this truly his fate? He'd come to the Wildlands for salvation, only to discover what he should've known all along.

He was doomed.

# Chapter 9

It was close to midnight when Rosalie was finally able to slip into the clinic unseen and catch Killian's guard on a quick trip to the bathroom. No doubt Raphael would kick her ass out of the Wildlands without a second thought if she got caught. But she didn't plan on getting caught. Breaking, entering, retrieving...it was what she lived for.

Inside his large room, the lights were dimmed enough that Rosalie could only make out shapes. The computer tables, covered lab equipment, monitors...bed. Her breathing surprisingly even, she moved swiftly and quietly toward it. No doubt he was fast asleep. Dreaming. Hopefully not the same nightmare she'd caught him in last night. She really didn't want to scare the shit out of him, but they didn't have much time. Her gut clenched momentarily as she wondered what kind of reception the human—no, *the male*—was going to give her after today's news regarding his permanent state of being. And what he believed to be her part in it. But she had to try. She owed him that much—

A sudden gasp ripped from her throat, but she stifled it by clamping a hand over her mouth. What the hell? Where...

She swallowed hard. The bed was empty.

In fact, it didn't looked slept in at all.

Her heart plummeted into her stomach. This was bad. Really bad. He'd escaped? How was that possible? Well, he was military...But where could he have gone? Wherever it was, she had to find him before Parish or one of the Hunters did. They didn't know what was going on. What he was. They'd just assume he was either an out of control human, or an out of control puma.

She turned and headed for the door only to be stopped in her tracks by six-plus feet of hard muscle, sinister expression, and shimmering blue shark eyes.

Her heart stuttered inside her chest. Was it possible that he had become a *male* in one day? Her gaze ran the length of him. He sure looked like one of them.

"K-killian...what are you...where were you..." she uttered like a scared fool. Which she was not. Refused to be. *Hunter, female. You're a fucking hardass Hunter. Act like it!*

"Couldn't sleep," he said.

His voice was husky, like his cat's growl, and it made her entire body tense. Flare with a heat she refused to acknowledge. It sounded hungry, demanding. Goddess, she remembered that sound. When Raphael had called her back to the cage, to a crazed puma who had instantly calmed and softened the moment she'd wrapped her hands around the bars and given him her attention.

"I'm not surprised," she said. "Sleeping in here can't be easy."

His eyes dropped to her mouth, making everything south of her navel stir. "Not in the mood for any new nightmares."

"Sure. Of course." Why did she sound so breathless?

Those eyes lifted to connect with hers. "Unless I do what you do to block them out."

She licked her dry lips. What the hell was happening to her? Every inch of her skin was tight. Hot. Ready to be touched. "I think you should wait on that. Shifting is an art. Takes practice to master."

"Is that why you're here, Hunter?" he asked with just a touch of sarcasm. One dark brow lifted. "To teach me?"

Her sex actually clenched at his words. Dammit! She shook her head. Not here to teach him, anything. Right? Right? "I want to take you somewhere," she managed to push out.

Those brows drew together. "Why?" A growl rumbled in his chest. His very broad chest. "To finish the job you started on the bank?" Even in the dim light, she saw his eyes suddenly cloud over. "I just might let you."

Her heart clenched at his words this time. As she'd said to him once, she knew pain when she heard it. And fuck her, she heard it now. "Don't say shit like that."

He sniffed. "It's true."

"I don't care."

"I feel…"

"I know," she said, then added, "It's overwhelming and shocking and scary and you have no clue what you want or what this means."

His eyes were tightly fitted to hers. "Yeah. Something like that."

"I'm sorry, Killian." His nostrils flared at her use of his name. "For everything. How I attacked you on the bank. Treated you last night. Then, coming around in my puma…"

He shook his head. "You heard the tech and Raphael. It was already done. Sealed-fate kind of thing."

"Killian?"

His nostrils flared and a soft groan rumbled in his throat. "It's so weird having you call me that."

"You don't like it?"

"Shit, Hunter, of course I like it."

Her insides melted, both at his words and the soft lust reflected in his eyes. She reached for his hand. "Come with me? I want to show you something."

He nodded, even threaded his fingers with hers. "But how, Kitten? The guard's back."

Rosalie froze, inhaled. Yes, of course. How hadn't she caught that? *Maybe because you're so wrapped up in this male's scent, and his mouth, and his eyes...* "How did *you* know that?" she asked him.

"Clearly I have the scent thing now too." He smiled wickedly, his voice low. "By the way, I smelled you coming. Shit, I smelled you an hour ago when you started watching the guard."

Flames erupted inside her, and she wanted nothing more than to pull up on her toes and attack his mouth. That full, heavy bottom lip that would feel delicious between her teeth. But she forced herself to stay cool. "So, you're a real Pantera now, are you?"

He shrugged. "Not sure what I am," he said, leaning in. "I'm curious. What do you want to show me, Kitten?"

Oh, the things that instantly came to her mind. She nearly started purring. "Might have to wait. At least until the guard needs to go to the bathroom again. Or when they have a shift change."

He gave her an almost arrogant look, then pulled on her hand. "Come on, Hunter."

"You know you can call me Rosalie now," she said, going with him. *I want you to. Want to hear my name on your lips. Maybe when you kiss me...*

"I think I'm used to Hunter now," he said. "Or Kitten. We'll see." He led her past the bank of lab equipment and computers, into the darkness, to a concealed door she'd never seen before.

"What is this?" she asked, suddenly yanked from her sexual haze into all business. Hunter business.

"A small office attached to the room." He opened the door. "Hidden."

She moved inside quickly, stealthily, and started checking out the space. Plain walls, office furniture, computers, bank of windows. Heavy moonlight. "How did you find it?"

He laughed softly, and said, "Combat Search and Rescue, Kitten," like that explained everything. And maybe to a human it would. Or a military-type human.

To Rosalie, it just sounded unbearably sexy.

"Ready?"

Her gaze flew to the window. He was already there; had the thing unlocked and open.

Yes. Very sexy.

"You'd make a damn fine Hunter," she said with a bit of a growl, slipping past him.

"Come on."

"Just sayin'."

They dropped down onto the damp earth, and before Killian could even question her about where they were going, Rosalie took off into the night, motioning for him to follow.

\* \* \* \*

"What is this?" Killian asked, his confused gaze trained on the moonlit cottage surrounded by cypress.

Rosalie came to stand beside him. She couldn't believe she'd actually come here, brought someone here. Especially a man. *A male.* She couldn't believe her cat had allowed it. That it hadn't fought her on it. In fact, the puma was so quiet, Rosalie almost didn't feel it breathing inside her. It was incredibly strange.

And yet, she was grateful.

"This is the house of a friend of mine," she said, her eyes running over the dark green paint and white trim.

There was a moment of silence. Just the wind blowing in the trees and night sounds of the animals. Then Killian asked, "A good friend?"

"Yeah."

Another pause. "More than a friend?"

She turned to look at him then. This male standing beside her as she paid her respects and said her good-byes. Killian was tall, strong, handsome, brave. A good male. A Pantera, for all intents and purposes. And she wanted him to know her—as more than just the angry puma chick who was out for human blood. She wanted him to know her as a female. "His name was Mercier," she said as he turned to look at her, too. "He was my mate."

Killian's nostrils flared instantly, and his eyes darkened. "Was?"

Rosalie nodded, tears in her throat. She wasn't a crier. Especially lately. She hadn't allowed herself that pleasure since she'd returned from the lab. Didn't feel like she was worthy. But they were coming now. Whether she'd welcomed them or not. "He and I were taken to one of the labs by some piece-of-shit humans," she explained. "We managed to escape, but…" Her voice broke. "Mercier was killed. Trying to protect me."

"Fuck…" Killian uttered on a breath. "No wonder…"

"I was blaming you because you were human. I was blaming you because I couldn't contain all the anger I felt. I was blaming you because…" Her voice broke. Again. And tears filled her eyes. "I was attracted to you."

His eyes filled with sadness and warmth. And understanding. "I'm sorry, Hunter."

"Please," she begged, her eyes pleading with him. "It's Rosalie. I don't want to be a Hunter to you."

A soft smile touched his mouth. "What do you want to be to me?"

The Wildlands seemed to grow quiet in that moment, as he stared at her, wondering, waiting. And she tried to gather her courage—the kind that came not from physical strength and power, but from being vulnerable.

She bit her lip. "A friend?" she whispered, though it sounded more like a question for him to answer. *Don't do this, Rosalie. Don't be a liar. His friendship is the last thing you want.*

"Walk with me?" She didn't wait for his answer. Just reached for his hand and started walking out of the trees and down to the bank—away from the house. It was time. To be thankful for the past, but to put it behind her too. "I can help you," she said to him as she headed for the bank of the bayou. "I can help you figure out how to shift, how to control your cat."

She scented his reticence before he even uttered the words, "I don't know."

She looked up at him as they walked. "What does that mean?"

His jaw was tight, his gaze predatory. He was looking more like a Pantera male with every second that passed.

Or maybe it was her. How she was seeing him. How her heart was seeing him…in a new light.

"I don't know if I want that," he said. "I don't know what I want. Where I belong. Is it true you can't shift outside the Wildlands?"

A hum started inside her. Loud and painful. *Outside.* Was that what he was thinking of doing? Leaving? Even after knowing what he was? What he'd become? "It's true," she said. "But I don't know about your...situation. You could be different."

He sniffed. "I'm most definitely different. I have to figure out where I belong now. *If* I belong anywhere."

"Don't talk like that," she said passionately.

"After what's happened today, how can I not?"

She cut him off, stood in front of him. Moonlight washed over his handsome face. "If you wanted to stay here, you could. I know Raphael would allow it."

He cursed, looked anywhere but at her. When he spotted a massive cypress down near the bayou, he left her and headed straight for it. Rosalie watched as he went over and sat down, pressed his back to the thick trunk.

She didn't want him to leave. This male she'd tried to push away, hate, hurt... She wanted him to stay in the Wildlands. With her. See what happened. Maybe heal from their respective pasts together.

But she wasn't going to ask him or push him.

Rubbing the chill from her skin, she went over to the tree and sat down beside him. She was quiet. Watched the bayou dance against the bank in the moonlight as she breathed in his scent and felt the warmth of him against her side.

"I don't want to be somewhere because I'm allowed to be there," Killian said after a few minutes had passed.

"I know," Rosalie said.

"I want to feel wanted. I want a home. After losing my family, my military career, I just want a home."

Her heart squeezed painfully, because, Goddess, so did she. A home. And all that it meant. So much more than just four walls and a roof. She'd wanted it for so long, she'd refused to admit it—or even acknowledge its possibility. "I understand," she said softly.

"But it sounds pathetic, right? Weak?"

"No!" She turned to him, scrambling to her knees. "No way." She shook her head, eyes imploring him. "When I said I understood about wanting a home, I do." She closed her eyes for a second and sighed. "I'm really sorry, Killian. For the way I treated you. What you saw...how I acted...that's not who I am." *Or who I want to be.* "Except for maybe—" She cut herself off, bit her lip.

"Except for what?" he asked, his expression intent.

*Last night.*

*Kissing you.*
*Feeling happy for the first time in a long time.*
*Not needing the puma to breathe.*

His eyes were blazing down into hers, trying to read her mind, her heart, and her soul. She wanted him to see it—all of it. And she nearly did. But something happened...inside of her—and it wasn't the cat. A fear of rejection? Of losing someone she cared for—again? Whatever it was crept in, took hold, and stole her vulnerability.

She turned away, back to the tree. "Look up, Killian," she said as her heart threatened to break out of her chest. "Look at those stars."

His eyes were on her for the longest time. Or it felt that way. The weight of those blue orbs... How long could she last before she gave in...and just—broke?

Then he turned.

Slipped his arm around her.

And as she exhaled weightily, he pulled her close and gave his attention to the sky.

# Chapter 10

The dreams that came at him now were nothing like they'd been. There was no death. No pain. No one to rescue. In fact, it was him who was being rescued. By green eyes and healing hands. Urgent whispers and a wild mouth.

The Hunter.

Kitten.

Rosalie.

Bright warmth soothed the backs of his eyelids and a breeze blew crisp over his skin. He groaned at the fucking wonder of it all.

And the wonder groaned back.

What the hell...? Eyes rocketing open, Killian looked around sharply. It was habit. Enemy could be anywhere. But there was no enemy here. Only grass and trees, wide bayou, and a very naked female kissing her way down his torso. Along with his cock, every inch of him hardened. It was the very female who'd ripped him from the water, then from his nightmares. The female who'd made him smile and hope, despair, then hope again. The female who made him want to...stay...

He groaned as she lapped at his navel with her tongue.

What was his name again?

"Morning," she whispered, her eyes flipping up to meet his as her fingers eased down his sweats.

Seriously? They were going to do this—

*Fuck!* His cock popped right out, hard as the trunk of the cypress above him. "Tell me this isn't a dream," he said gruffly, taking in her soft, tanned curves. She was the most incredible sight. Perfection. Seduction. Bathed in soft yellow, the sun coming up behind her...

She smiled at him, then wrapped her hand around his erection and kissed the tip. "Does that feel like a dream?"

He groaned, his ass tightening. "Fuck yeah."

She laughed, then started to stroke him. Up. Down. Soft palm, warm fingers. "I've been thinking about this since dawn."

*Shit.* It was like the perfect pressure. He sucked air through his teeth and jacked up his hips. "Next time, don't think," he growled. "Or wait."

"Next time?" she purred.

Teeth gritted, body rigid, his eyes captured hers and held. Was that hope he saw there? She wanted a next time? More? Him? This? Or his own hope mirrored back? He needed to know. Had to know...

But the question died as his brain started to spin. After stroking him, up and over, then down to the base, Rosalie guided his cock to her lips. Her eyes still clinging to his, she very slowly drew him in.

Instantly, Killian started to move. Thrust. Shit, he couldn't help himself. Her mouth was so hot, her eyes, too—and her tongue was pressing against the base of his shaft. Christ, what was that? He felt like his dick was drowning in pure pleasure.

She made sounds too. Soft growls, hisses, moans of hunger. And as she took him all the way to the back of her throat, over and over, Killian tried like hell to tamp down his need to either come or get her on her back and fuck her until they both exploded. But it was impossible. As she continued to blow the living hell out of him, drawing him in and out of her sexy mouth, she lifted her ass up in the air and was wiggling it, back and forth. Like it had a fucking tail on it.

Mind gone.

Balls tight and ready.

He. Was. So. Going. To. Have. Her.

And not alone. The thing inside him. The puma—*his puma*—wanted her, too.

She released him for a moment, to yank his sweats down to his knees. It was the opportunity both Killian and his cat had been waiting for. He was up and pressing her back to the ground in seconds. As he loomed over her, a snarl exited his throat. The cat was with him, inside him, wanting, needing, hungry... *Was this normal?* he wondered, grabbing her legs. Did the cat and the male coexist? Feed together? Fuck together?

Well, he was going to find out.

He pressed her knees to her chest, then stared down at what he'd created. A perfect feast. Rosalie gazed up at him, looking feral and excited and ready. Her eyes were wide and bright; her mouth wet and curved up into a challenging smile.

*Yes, Kitten, you'll get as good as you give.*

It was the last thing Killian thought for a full minute as he dove between her legs and fed off her hot, juicy pussy. She was shaved bare and her scent... Christ, her scent. It was a drug he would never quit. A welcome addiction.

She was his. His and the puma's.

Now he just had to make her see it too.

Her fingers were threading in his hair, fisting, then scraping his scalp as he flicked her swollen clitoris with his tongue. She liked it fast and light. Every time he changed the rhythm, her hold on him slackened, so he kept it up, just right, perfect—until her nails dug into his scalp.

*That's right, Hunter, make me bleed.*

As she fucked his mouth, thrusting and grinding, he watched her. She was unbearably beautiful. She was watching him too. Her skin pink, her mouth parted, panting, her eyes at half-mast, her brow furrowed as she neared orgasm.

The puma was whispering something to him. It was the only way Killian could describe the sensation. *Suck. Suck her like she sucked you...*

Without question, he wrapped his lips around her clit and drew her in. Rosalie went wild. Crying out, writhing, releasing his head and grabbing her perfect breasts, pinching her nipples as he continued to suckle her. Come leaked from the tip of Killian's dick, but he only sought her climax. And with one deep pull, she broke open. Her body tensed and as her clit swelled against his tongue, he sucked her, taking each beat, each moan of orgasm into his mind and heart and skin, and offering it to the being that had given him this.

This female's pleasure.

Their female's pleasure.

Rosalie barely gave her climax time to ease before she groaned the words, "Inside me. You. Inside me. Now."

As insane and hungry as Killian felt, he couldn't help but grin. He loved this. This female who said what she wanted, was tough and strong, but sensual and female at the same time.

He pulled away and rose over her. She was ready for him, wrapping her legs around his hips the very second he had his cock at her entrance—and pulling him down for a kiss the second he pushed inside of her.

No. Killian was no longer a man. He'd felt the switch. Last night. This morning. It all ran together. He was a male. A shifter.

*Hers...*

Hot desire flooded him and he could do nothing else but move. Deep, possessive thrusts as he slipped his hands beneath her ass and kissed her. Around them, the sun was streaking through the treetops, illuminating their bond.

Something stunning was happening inside Killian. The pain that had once landed and taken root within him was trying to break free. Fear and guilt couldn't survive where there was this…him and Rosalie. There wasn't room to house it.

Pulling his mouth from hers, he eased back so he could see her. The stunning female that was his. All that yellow hair, spread out around her gorgeous face. Lips wet and pink from his kiss. Cheeks flushed. Neck strained as another orgasm built inside her. Heavy breasts bouncing with each hard thrust.

He shook his head. "The perfect rose. I understand your name now." He sucked air between his teeth as her hot walls tightened around his cock. "Beautiful, soft, proud and a scent so intoxicating, I want to get drunk every fucking night."

That elicited a wide grin and a soft laugh interspersed with gasps as he gave her three punishing thrusts.

He pulled one hand from her backside and reached between them, brushed his thumb over her still-swollen clit. Instantly, she cried out.

"Like that, Kitten?"

She nodded, her breath labored. "Goddess, yes."

As he gazed into her eyes, he brought the pad of his thumb to his mouth and licked her cream. *Perfection.* "This is what I like."

Before she could say another word, or even make a sound, his thumb was back on her clit, and he was pumping inside her brutally fast. Her eyes closed and her nostrils flared. The combination was too much. Once again, she broke, flying over the edge of happiness and pleasure. Bucking wildly, squeezing against his dick.

And Killian wasn't about to be left behind. Sweat on his brow, every muscle straining, he moved, driving into her, over and over, until…

"Oh, fuck!" he snarled, thrusting deep and holding as he released a wash of come inside her.

"Rose," he uttered, then pulled her into his arms, rolling them to one side. Still connected, he held her both possessively and protectively. *I'm never letting you go. You're mine. Mine.*

For long moments, they lay there on the cool ground, under the dappled morning sun and fragrant flora, touching and tasting, stroking and kissing. Rosalie's leg was tossed over Killian's hip and his hand was cupping her ass.

"What is this?" she asked, running her nails over the black barren tree with the words *"There is no secret here"* interwoven in branches tattooed on his shoulder.

"A reminder," he uttered between kisses to her neck.

"Of what?" Her voice carried the delectable strains of jealousy.

He eased back, looked at her, smiled gently. "To never leave things unsaid. If you care about someone, love someone, make sure they know it."

A soft growl rumbled in her chest. "Was it for a female?" she asked, yanking him closer with her leg. "In your past?"

His cock pulsed, started to harden inside her once again. Oh, they were going to have fun together. Painful sometimes, pleasure always. He grinned at her. "A female inspired it."

Her eyes narrowed, and that growl became a snarl.

"Easy, Kitten," he said, then gave her one deep kiss. "She wasn't my female," he whispered against her lips. "She was the wife of a Ranger I wasn't able to save. A guy who hadn't been able to say good-bye or I love you."

Her entire being changed. "Oh." And her eyes softened.

He didn't know which Rosalie he adored more. The possessive she-cat or the soft, supple female. He leaned in and kissed her gently on the mouth. "Come on, baby. You're the only female I—"

Killian froze. Rosalie too, as the sound of movement in the undergrowth caught their ears. It wasn't a random skunk or possum. It was predatory. It was Pantera.

*Hunter.*

Rosalie was the first to scramble away and leap to her feet. Naked and flushed from sex, she crouched into a fighting stance. His cock hard against his abdomen, Killian moved in front of her. But something was happening. To him. To the world around him. Eyes growing sharper, scent intensifying... No! But before he could stop it, his mind receded and he was no longer the Ranger, the man—or the male.

He was puma.

The puma who would kill anything or anyone who even looked at his female.

# Chapter 11

"Just say what you have to say." Rosalie stood near the border of the Wildlands. It was midday and warm for winter, and she was about to be kicked out on her ass. Had to be. Killian was still breathing, but shit, she'd broken every rule in the Pantera book, and now she was going to have to live with the consequences.

Raphael and Parish stood before her. The judgment police. Giving her the stink eye and a formal good-bye. After, of course, a thorough dressing down about the many ways she'd screwed up in the past couple of days.

"What if he'd taken off?" Parish demanded, his gold eyes furious. "We don't know what he's capable of. What if he can shift outside of the Wildlands? What if he'd gotten hurt? Or hurt a human?"

"I wouldn't have let that happen." Even as she said the words, she knew they were useless.

"You're reckless," Parish said.

"And arrogant," Raphael finished.

"Better than angry," she tossed back. "Or miserable or guilty or bitter."

Neither male said a word to that. Just stared at her. Clearly, it wasn't the reply they'd expected. For the twenty-four/seven puma female to realize—no, to admit that she'd been anything but *fine* over the past several months.

She took a deep breath, looked to her right at the beautiful Wildlands, her home since she knew what home was. Killian was in there, somewhere, probably back at the clinic, recovering from the tranquilizer dart Parish had shot him with. Bastard. Forget about her cat's insane reaction, she'd nearly lost her mind when the leader of the Hunter's had done that.

She felt their eyes on her. Waiting. Needing an explanation. Her heart squeezed painfully. "When Mercier was killed," she started, almost as if she was speaking to herself, "I truly thought I'd never feel hopeful again. Maybe because I didn't think I deserved to feel it. Not when he couldn't. But now I know that kind of thinking doesn't honor his memory at all. It defiles it." She turned back to face the two males who held her future, at least in the Wildlands, in their hands. "I know what I did was wrong. For you, Raphael, according to the rules and the promises I made, I wouldn't blame you…"

"Rules are there for a reason, Hunter," Parish said tightly, though his eyes weren't nearly as hostile as they were a moment ago. "We can't function as a society without them."

"I get that," she said. "But this time, this rule breaking, it wasn't wrong for me or for Killian. It saved us both, I think. I don't regret it."

"Oh, shit," Parish ground out.

"I'm prepared to go," Rosalie continued, her chin lifted proudly, though inside she was wilting. "Not into the regular world, of course. I couldn't stand that for long."

"Then where?" Raphael asked, his expression thick with concern.

"Hiss and his mate are in the Wetlands. I'm hoping I'll be welcome there."

The scent of him came seconds before the voice.

*Killian.*

He came through the brush with two Hunters, Ice and Keira, Parish's twin sister. He was all male, not a prisoner or a tagalong. He was flanked by both Hunters, as if he was one of them. A smile came to Rosalie's lips as pride touched her heart. He looked so right with them.

"You're not going anywhere," he said, though his blue shark eyes were trained on Raphael.

"This is between us and Rosalie," the leader of the Pantera told him with an edge.

The once human man, who seemed utterly and completely Pantera now, shook his head. "She's not leaving the Wildlands, Raphael."

"That's not for you to say," the male told him.

"You offered me a home here," Killian countered, stepping forward, coming to stand beside Rosalie.

"Yes."

"And if I wanted to take a mate, she would also be welcome here."

"Of course, but—"

"Well, I took one."

Rosalie's growl broke over the border, and she turned on Killian and snarled out her demand, "Who. Did. You. Mate?"

He stared into her eyes and grinned. Wide. Rosalie bristled, and her cat backed down. Unbelievable. Not only wasn't he afraid of her wrath, claws, puma, or fangs—he was turned on.

She could scent it.

Her lip curled.

*Males.*

"Answer me, Human," she hissed, pressing up against him. Oh yeah, definitely turned on.

He licked his lower lip and a rumble sounded in his chest. "Goddamn, I love it when you call me Human," he said. "Don't think my cat does though."

"Who did you mate, damn you?" she nearly cried.

The smile on his face and his eyes died. He looked at her like she was crazy. "Jesus, Hunter. It's you, for fuck's sake. You're my mate."

She must've gone both pale and blank because Keira and Ice started laughing. She turned on them and snarled. Which only made them laugh harder.

"Fuck the both of you," she spat. "And you." She turned back to address Killian. "I never gave myself to you." She lifted her chin, trying to act all cool and haughty, when secretly, relief and happiness were pouring through her. Such a phony.

Killian cocked one eyebrow and said in a voice for all to hear. "You want me to go over the many ways you gave yourself to me? Now, I don't give a shit if these four hear it, but you might." He grinned wickedly, and those blue eyes flashed. "I'm going to be very detailed, Kitten."

Her body responded instantly, erupting into flame, and she leapt at him—wrapped her arms around his neck. Her heart pounding with the wondrous rhythm of new love, she kissed him. Hungrily. Desperately. Hopefully. When she pulled back, she eyed him and growled against his wet lips, "Ask me, Killian."

He knew exactly what she meant, what she wanted. His hold on her tightened. "Be my mate, Rosalie?"

She smiled back. "All right."

"And my home?"

"Sure."

"And my heart?"

"Okay."

"And my partner in all things Pantera?" His expression downgraded to grim. "If there's one of me, the super solider, then there are more."

She nodded solemnly. "I'm with you. All the way. By your side."

His eyes warmed with the kind of happiness that only came from feeling understood and cared for.

"Us too," Keira called out. "It's about time we went on another field trip."

"Fuck yeah," Ice agreed.

But Killian and Rosalie weren't listening. Killian had pulled her even tighter to him, and was uttering against her mouth, "And you'll help me figure out the shifting thing? How to control—"

Rosalie shut him up with a hard, hungry kiss. She was his and he was hers. And all she wanted in that moment was to revel in the beauty of forgiveness, and letting go of fear and guilt. Her hands drove into his hair, and he growled and sucked on her tongue. At some point, she ripped her mouth away from his to tell the four suddenly silent Pantera to go away—that they could kick her ass out later.

Parish grumbled of course. And Raphael said in his most authoritative tone, "We'll have a strategy session tomorrow at noon. And I *will* see you both there." But they left.

Because really, no one messes with a Pantera female in love.

Except maybe the male, the mate, who loves her in return.

Sign up for the 1001 Dark Nights Newsletter
and be entered to win a Tiffany Key necklace.

There's a contest every month!

Go to www.1001DarkNights.com to subscribe.

As a bonus, all subscribers will receive a free
1001 Dark Nights story
*The First Night*
by Lexi Blake & M.J. Rose

Turn the page for a full list of the
1001 Dark Nights fabulous novellas...

# 1001 DARK NIGHTS

WICKED WOLF by Carrie Ann Ryan
A Redwood Pack Novella

WHEN IRISH EYES ARE HAUNTING by Heather Graham
A Krewe of Hunters Novella

EASY WITH YOU by Kristen Proby
A With Me In Seattle Novella

MASTER OF FREEDOM by Cherise Sinclair
A Mountain Masters Novella

CARESS OF PLEASURE by Julie Kenner
A Dark Pleasures Novella

ADORED by Lexi Blake
A Masters and Mercenaries Novella

HADES by Larissa Ione
A Demonica Novella

RAVAGED by Elisabeth Naughton
An Eternal Guardians Novella

DREAM OF YOU by Jennifer L. Armentrout
A Wait For You Novella

STRIPPED DOWN by Lorelei James
A Blacktop Cowboys ® Novella

RAGE/KILLIAN by Alexandra Ivy/Laura Wright
Bayou Heat Novellas

DRAGON KING by Donna Grant
A Dark Kings Novella

PURE WICKED by Shayla Black
A Wicked Lovers Novella

HARD AS STEEL by Laura Kaye
A Hard Ink/Raven Riders Crossover

STROKE OF MIDNIGHT by Lara Adrian
A Midnight Breed Novella

ALL HALLOWS EVE by Heather Graham
A Krewe of Hunters Novella

KISS THE FLAME by Christopher Rice
A Desire Exchange Novella

DARING HER LOVE by Melissa Foster
A Bradens Novella

TEASED by Rebecca Zanetti
A Dark Protectors Novella

THE PROMISE OF SURRENDER by Liliana Hart
A MacKenzie Family Novella

FOREVER WICKED by Shayla Black
A Wicked Lovers Novella

CRIMSON TWILIGHT by Heather Graham
A Krewe of Hunters Novella

CAPTURED IN SURRENDER by Liliana Hart
A MacKenzie Family Novella

SILENT BITE: A SCANGUARDS WEDDING by Tina Folsom
A Scanguards Vampire Novella

DUNGEON GAMES by Lexi Blake
A Masters and Mercenaries Novella

AZAGOTH by Larissa Ione
A Demonica Novella

NEED YOU NOW by Lisa Renee Jones
A Shattered Promises Series Prelude

SHOW ME, BABY by Cherise Sinclair
A Masters of the Shadowlands Novella

ROPED IN by Lorelei James
A Blacktop Cowboys ® Novella

TEMPTED BY MIDNIGHT by Lara Adrian
A Midnight Breed Novella

THE FLAME by Christopher Rice
A Desire Exchange Novella

CARESS OF DARKNESS by Julie Kenner
A Dark Pleasures Novella


*Also from Evil Eye Concepts:*

TAME ME by J. Kenner
A Stark International Novella

THE SURRENDER GATE By Christopher Rice
A Desire Exchange Novel

SERVICING THE TARGET By Cherise Sinclair
A Masters of the Shadowlands Novel

# About the Authors

Alexandra Ivy is a *New York Times* and *USA Today* bestselling author of the Guardians of Eternity, as well as the Sentinels, Dragons of Eternity and ARES series. After majoring in theatre she decided she prefers to bring her characters to life on paper rather than stage. She lives in Missouri with her family. Visit her website at alexandraivy.com.

New York Times and USA Today Bestselling Author, Laura Wright is passionate about romantic fiction. Though she has spent most of her life immersed in acting, singing and competitive ballroom dancing, when she found the world of writing and books and endless cups of coffee she knew she was home. Laura is the author of the bestselling Mark of the Vampire series and the USA Today bestselling series, Bayou Heat, which she co-authors with Alexandra Ivy.

Laura lives in Los Angeles with her husband, two young children and three loveable dogs.

# Kill Without Mercy
Ares Security Book 1
By Alexandra Ivy
Coming December 29, 2015

From the hellhole of a Taliban prison to sweet freedom, five brave military heroes have made it home—and they're ready to take on the civilian missions no one else can. Individually they're intimidating. Together they're invincible. They're the men of ARES Security.

Rafe Vargas is only in Newton, Iowa, to clear out his late grandfather's small house. As the covert ops specialist for ARES Security, he's eager to get back to his new life in Texas. But when he crosses paths with Annie White, a haunted beauty with skeletons in her closet, he can't just walk away—not when she's clearly in danger…

There's a mysterious serial killer on the loose with a link to Annie's dark past. And the closer he gets, the deeper Rafe's instinct to protect kicks in. But even with his considerable skill, Annie's courage, and his ARES buddies behind him, the slaying won't stop. Now it's only a matter of time before Annie's next—unless they can unravel a history of deadly lies that won't be buried.

\* \* \* \*

Friday nights in Houston meant crowded bars, loud music and ice-cold beer. It was a tradition that Rafe and his friends had quickly adapted to suit their own tastes when they moved to Texas five months ago.

After all, none of them were into the dance scene. They were too old for half-naked coeds and casual hookups. And none of them wanted to have to scream over pounding music to have a decent conversation.

Instead, they'd found The Saloon, a small, cozy bar with lots of polished wood, a jazz band that played softly in the background, and a handful of locals who knew better than to bother the other customers. Oh, and the finest tequila in the city.

They even had their own table that was reserved for them every Friday night.

Tucked in a back corner, it was shrouded in shadows and well away from the long bar that ran the length of one wall. A perfect spot to observe without being observed.

And best of all, situated so no one could sneak up from behind.

It might have been almost two years since they'd returned from the war, but none of them had forgotten. Lowering your guard, even for a second, could mean death.

Lesson. Fucking. Learned.

Tonight, however, it was only Rafe and Hauk at the table, both of them sipping tequila and eating peanuts from a small bucket.

Lucas was still in Washington D.C., working his contacts to help drum up business for their new security business, ARES. Max had remained at their new offices, putting the final touches on his precious forensics lab, and Teagan was on his way to the bar after installing a computer system that would give Homeland Security a hemorrhage if they knew what he was doing.

Leaning back in his chair, Rafe intended to spend the night relaxing after a long week of hassling with the red tape and bullshit regulations that went into opening a new business, when he made the mistake of checking his messages.

"Shit."

He tossed his cellphone on the polished surface of the wooden table, a tangled ball of emotions lodged in the pit of his stomach.

Across the table Hauk sipped his tequila and studied Rafe with a lift of his brows.

At a glance, the two men couldn't be more different.

Rafe had dark hair that had grown long enough to touch the collar of his white button-down shirt along with dark eyes that were lushly framed by long, black lashes. His skin remained tanned dark bronze despite the fact it was late September, and his body was honed with muscles that came from working on the small ranch he'd just purchased, not the gym.

Hauk, on the other hand, had inherited his Scandinavian father's pale blond hair that he kept cut short, and brilliant blue eyes that held a cunning intelligence. He had a narrow face with sculpted features that were usually set in a stern expression.

And it wasn't just their outward appearance that made them so different.

Rafe was hot tempered, passionate and willing to trust his gut instincts.

Hauk was aloof, calculating, and mind-numbingly anal. Not that Hauk would admit he was OCD. He preferred to call himself detail-oriented.

Which was exactly why he was a successful sniper. Rafe, on the other hand, had been trained in combat rescue. He was capable of making quick decisions, and ready to change strategies on the fly.

"Trouble?" Hauk demanded.

Rafe grimaced. "The real estate agent left a message saying she has a buyer for my grandfather's house."

Hauk looked predictably confused. Rafe had been bitching about the need to get rid of his grandfather's house since the old man's death a year ago.

"Shouldn't that be good news?"

"It would be if I didn't have to travel to Newton to clean it out," Rafe said.

"Aren't there people you can hire to pack up the shit and send it to you?"

"Not in the middle of fucking nowhere."

Hauk's lips twisted into a humorless smile. "I've been in the middle of fucking nowhere, amigo, and it ain't Kansas," he said, the shadows from the past darkening his eyes.

"Newton's in Iowa, but I get your point," Rafe conceded. He did his best to keep the memories in the past where they belonged. Most of the time he was successful. Other times the demons refused to be leashed. "Okay, it's not the hell hole we crawled out of, but the town might as well be living in another century. I'll have to go deal with my grandfather's belongings myself."

Hauk reached to pour himself another shot of tequila from the bottle that had been waiting for them in the center of the table.

Like Rafe, he was dressed in an Oxford shirt, although his was blue instead of white, and he was wearing black dress pants instead of jeans.

"I know you think it's a pain, but it's probably for the best."

Rafe glared at his friend. The last thing he wanted was to drive a thousand miles to pack up the belongings of a cantankerous old man who'd never forgiven Rafe's father for walking away from Iowa. "Already trying to get rid of me?"

"Hell no. Of the five of us, you're the..."

"I'm afraid to ask," Rafe muttered as Hauk hesitated.

"The glue," he at last said.

Rafe gave a bark of laughter. He'd been called a lot of things over the years. Most of them unrepeatable. But glue was a new one. "What the hell does that mean?"

Hauk settled back in his seat. "Lucas is the smooth-talker, Max is the heart, Teagan is the brains and I'm the organizer." The older man shrugged. "You're the one who holds us all together. ARES would never have happened without you."

Rafe couldn't argue. After returning to the States, the five of them had been transferred to separate hospitals to treat their numerous injuries. It would have been easy to drift apart. The natural instinct was to avoid anything that could remind them of the horror they'd endured.

But Rafe had quickly discovered that returning to civilian life wasn't a simple matter of buying a home and getting a 9-to-5 job.

He couldn't bear the thought of being trapped in a small cubicle eight hours a day, or returning to an empty condo that would never be a home.

It felt way too much like the prison he'd barely escaped.

# Bonded
## The Cavanaugh Brothers Book 4
### By Laura Wright
### Coming September 1, 2015

*The New York Times bestselling author of Brash returns to the Triple C Ranch in River Black, Texas, for more cowboys, romance, and danger...*

Ranch hand Blue Perez's once simple life is spinning out of control. He's discovered he has three half-brothers, and they're not ready to accept his claim on the ranch. Also, Blue's girlfriend may have betrayed him in the worst way possible. And after one evening of drowning his sorrows at the bar, there's someone he can't get out of his mind, a woman who says she's carrying his child.

Following a night of breathtaking passion in the arms of the man she's longed for all her life, waitress Emily Shiver is contemplating her next step. With everything that's going on in Blue's life, she doesn't want to force him into fatherhood. Yet as hard hearted as he may seem, Blue can't turn his back on her, particularly when she becomes the target of someone's dark obsession....

\* \* \* \*

Last thing she wanted was someone getting hurt because of her. Especially someone with such a beautiful face. That hard, sexy jawline . . .

This time when she rolled her eyes it was internal and at herself.

She reached for a napkin on the table behind her. "Your lip . . . Let me clean it up for you."

"Naw, it's nothing."

"You're bleeding," she said.

He swiped at his lip and the blood with the back of his hand. "All gone."

"Well, that wasn't very sanitary," she said.

His eyes, those incredible blue eyes, warmed with momentary humor. Then he touched the brim of his hat and turned to head back to the bar. "Ma'am."

Emily stared after him, confused. What was that? Saves the day and on his way? "Hey, hold on a sec," she called out. "I didn't thank you."

"There's no need," he called back, sliding onto the same barstool he'd occupied earlier.

Well, that's not very neighborly, she mused. She followed him. "Maybe not," she said, coming up to stand beside him. "But I'm going to do it anyway."

He turned to look at her but didn't say anything. Good night, nurse, he was handsome.

She inclined her head formally. "Thank you."

Those incredible eyes moved over her face then. So probing, so thoughtful. They made her toes curl inside her shoes. "Something tells me you could've taken those men out yourself."

"What tells you that?" she asked.

He ran a hand over his jaw, which was darkening by the minute. "Just a guess."

Her gaze flickered to the bruise, to his mouth, and she frowned. "Are you in pain?"

"Constantly," he said, then turned back to his drink.

The strange, almost morose response made her pause. But before she could ask him anything about it, Dean slid back behind the bar and asked, "You want something, Em? After having to deal with those assholes I'd say you're done for the night. But first, a drink."

"And it's on me," Blue said, then tossed back his tequila.

Dean gave the cowboy a broad grin. "After what you did for our girl here, it's me who's buying."

"Well, thank you kindly." Blue held up his empty glass. "Another, if you please. And what would you like . . . ?" He turned to Emily and arched a brow at her. "Em, is it?"

The soft masculine growl in his voice made her insides warm. "Emily," she told him. "Emily Shiver."

"Right." He cocked his head to one side and studied her. "The girl with the flowers in her hair," he said, his gaze catching on the yellow one behind her ear.

Emily smiled. Couldn't help it. She liked that he'd noticed. "Started when I was little," she told him. "Stole flowers from my grandmother's garden every time I was over there. I'd put them everywhere. My room, the tables here, in my hair." She shrugged. "It became kind of an obsession."

His gaze flickered to the flower in her hair again, then returned to her face. "Pretty."

Heat instantly spread through Emily's insides. Granted, plenty of men came into the Bull's Eye and looked at her with eyes heavy on the hungry—either for food or for her. Hell, sometimes both. But no one had ever looked at her like Blue was now. Curious, frustrated, interested . . .

"Drink, Em?"

Swallowing hard, she turned to see a waiting and mildly curious Dean. "Just a Coke for me, boss. Thanks."

Blue groaned as Dean filled a glass with ice.

"What's wrong?" Emily asked him, wondering if his jaw was paining him.

But the man just chuckled softly. "Come on, now. Have something a little stronger than that.

You're gonna make me feel bad. Or worse." Under his breath he added, "If that's even possible tonight."

Curiosity coiled within her at his words. The way he looked at her, spoke, acted . . . clearly he was working through some heavy feelings tonight. Was it about the fight with the jerkweeds? Or something that came before it? She bit her lip. Did she ask? Or did she wait for him to tell her? But why would he tell her? They barely knew each other.

Maybe she should just ignore it . . .

Dean set the Coke before her and poured another round of tequila for Blue, which the cowboy drained in about five seconds flat; then he tapped the bar top to indicate he wanted another.

Oh yeah. Definitely dealing with something. She'd worked at the Bull's Eye long enough to know that drinking like he was doing had nothing to do with relaxing after a long day. Dark feelings were running through Blue Perez's blood. And maybe some demons to go along with them.

"Everything all right tonight, cowboy?" she asked.

"Yep." He turned to look at her again, his gaze not all that sharp or engaged now. The liquor was starting to do its thing. "I remember you. Flowers, and a ton of strawberry blond curls."

Emily's breath caught inside her lungs. What a strange and very suggestive thing to say. Not that she minded. Just wished he'd have said it before the double shot. And the way he was staring at her . . . like he was trying to memorize her features or something. Then suddenly, he reached out and touched her hair, fingered one of those curls caught up in a ponytail.

A hot, powerful shiver moved up her spine.

"Here you go," Dean interrupted, filling Blue's glass once again.

"Thanks," Blue said, though his eyes were still on Emily. Even when his fingers curled around the glass, his eyes remained locked with hers. "Sure you don't want something stronger, Em?" he asked.

Emily's brows shot up, and her belly clenched with awareness. "I think you're doing fine for the both of us," she said, reaching for her Coke and taking a sip. Her mouth was incredibly dry. "And I'm going to assume that you'll be walking home."

He downed the contents of the glass and chuckled. "Not to worry, darlin'. I got my truck."

Oh jeez. Not to worry? She shook her head. People could be so stupid sometimes. So reckless. Even gorgeous cowboys with eyes the color of a cloudless Texas sky— and a pair of lips that kept calling to her own.

Like the meddlesome gal she was, she reached over and grabbed his keys off the bar top. Blue's gaze turned sharply to hers, and under the heat of that electric stare, Emily tried not to melt. Well, outwardly at any rate.

*Yes, you're hot and sexy and annoyed at my ass now. But I'm not going to let you be a shit for brains.*

She held up the keys. "No rush, cowboy. I got my Coke here, and nowhere to get to. I'm going to take you home when you've sufficiently drowned yourself."

Blue didn't like that one bit. He released a breath and ground out, "Not necessary."

"I say it is," she returned.

"You don't want to do that, darlin'. I'm not fit to be around tonight."

"Maybe not. But there's no use arguing the matter. I always win arguments. Right, Dean?"

The bartender chuckled. "Don't even try anymore."

"If you're really going to push this, I can call someone—" Blue started, then stopped. His eyes came up and met hers, and it was impossible to miss the heavy, pulsing pain that echoed there.

This wasn't about the jerks or a bad day. This was deep and long lasting. Emily knew some of what had happened to him in the past couple of months. Finding out— along with the whole town— that his daddy was Everett Cavanaugh. That he had part claim to the Triple C. Along with a set of three new brothers. But clearly there was more that was weighing on him. So much more, she'd venture to guess.

She slipped the keys into her jeans pocket and settled back in front of her Coke. This wasn't how she'd wanted the night to go. Watching over a hot, drunk cowboy. She'd had visions of a bathtub, a great book, and some buttered noodles afterward. But tonight this man had offered up his protection, and she couldn't help but do the same.

## On behalf of 1001 Dark Nights,

Liz Berry and M.J. Rose would like to thank ~

Steve Berry
Doug Scofield
Kim Guidroz
Jillian Stein
InkSlinger PR
Dan Slater
Asha Hossain
Chris Graham
Pamela Jamison
Jessica Johns
Dylan Stockton
Richard Blake
BookTrib After Dark
The Dinner Party Show
and Simon Lipskar